Murder Is Collegiate

A Susan Wiles Schoolhouse Mystery

by

Diane Weiner

For information, email Cozy Cat Press,

cozycatpress@aol.com or visit our website at: www.cozycatpress.com

COZY CAT
P R E S S

ISBN: 978-1-939816-92-4

Printed in the United States of America

Cover by Paula Ellenberger
http://www.paulaellenberger.com/design

1 2 3 4 5 6 7 8 9 10

This book is dedicated to my stepmother, Laura Grigull, in appreciation for the love, patience, and dedication she showed my father when he needed her the most.

Chapter 1

"Look at this place. No wonder it's listed in that book about places to visit before you die," said Susan Wiles. "I haven't been this far north in Vermont before. Sugarbury Falls. Even the name is enticing. Maybe you should retire and we can move up here."

"I've got a few more years left in me," said Mike, her husband of nearly forty years. After a recent heart attack, he had cut back his hours at the city permits office in their hometown of Westbrook, New York, but wasn't ready to fully retire as Susan had. "It is beautiful. Emily and Henry are fortunate to have inherited the family cabin, especially since they both love hiking and skiing."

Susan said, "And lucky enough to be able to afford to retire. Henry worked a lot of hours at the hospital. Good for him, he socked away part of his radiologist salary all along so he wouldn't have to work into his old age."

Mike turned onto a two-lane dirt road. A sprinkling of snow powdered the landscape. The pine trees looked like vanilla-frosted Christmas cupcakes, interspersed with the bare maples that fueled the town's economy. It was late February, and their newly-retired friends had warned them it would be colder than they were used to back in upstate New York. Susan turned up the heat in their blue Prius.

Susan was grateful for the escape from recent family events. She'd just met her birth father for the first time. Her birth mother had said he didn't know Susan existed, but in working to solve a case, Susan ultimately found out that her birth father, Jonathan Stirling, had put the pieces together and was thrilled to find he had a child. He planned to visit them next month.

"Look, Mike. Maplewood. That's their community." Mike slowed down when he encountered a fork in the road. "Doesn't this remind you of that Robert Frost poem?"

Mike chuckled. "Both sides look less traveled to me, but the directions say to go right." Farther down the road, he followed a hand-painted wooden sign that pointed in the direction of the Foxes' cabin. The road circled around a frozen lake that was sparsely dotted with wooden cabins.

"According to Emily's directions, it should be coming up on the left," said Susan. "There it is."

Mike turned onto a gravel driveway and parked in front of a quaint, wooden cabin. The welcome mat read, "The Foxes." Tied in place, red gingham curtains partially covered the windows. Susan knocked.

"No one's answering. Emily said they'd be home."

"Try again."

Susan knocked harder but still no response. She peeked through the window. "The lights are off. I don't think they're home. That's weird." She tried calling but couldn't get service. "Back home, they always kept a key hidden." She lifted the mat and picked up a silver key, which she inserted into the lock. "Voilà."

The inside of the cabin was cozily decorated and smelled like apple cinnamon. A plush sofa and two overstuffed chairs faced a stone fireplace, with a colorful quilt neatly folded on the hearth. A black creature leaped off the back of the sofa, startling Susan. She caught her breath and remembered the family pet.

"Chester! How do you like your new home?" Chester answered with a meow and ran into the kitchen.

Susan followed. "No one is in here. The coffee is set up, and dessert plates are stacked on the counter. She didn't forget we were coming."

They peeked into the downstairs guest room, and Mike climbed the ladder leading to the master bedroom loft. "No one's up here either."

As Mike descended, they heard a key turn in the door. A fiftyish man with neat gray hair came in holding a bakery box. "Susan, Mike! So glad you're here." He set the cake on the kitchen counter. "Emily, where are you?"

"She's not here," said Susan.

"Not here? She should have been home hours ago. She teaches a morning writing class over at St. Edwards College. Takes her ten minutes to get home when the roads are clear." He picked up the landline and dialed Emily's office. "No answer."

"Maybe she stopped at the grocery store," said Susan.

"She did the shopping yesterday. Sent me to the bakery to pick up a fresh dessert today."

"Maybe she got pulled into a meeting. My daughter's husband is a professor, and it happens to him all the time."

"Or maybe she had car trouble," offered Mike.

"I'm going over to the college. This isn't like her."

Mike and Susan followed Henry into the car. On the way out of Maplewood, they passed the Foxes' next-door neighbor, Kurt Olav. Kurt was a salty older gentleman with ice-blue eyes, who'd relocated to Sugarbury Falls from Minnesota. Henry motioned him to stop and rolled down the car window.

"Have you seen Emily?"

In a dragged-out monotone, he answered, "Haven't seen her all day though I thought I saw the barn door open as I was heading out earlier."

"Barn door? Emily never goes into the barn. I'll have to check the latch. It must have been the wind."

Henry continued to St. Edwards College, a small Gothic-style campus surrounded by dark woods. They parked outside a two-story, stone building and entered through a thick wooden door.

"Her office is right down the hall," said Henry. Susan and Mike followed, nearly crashing into him when he stopped abruptly in front of Emily's office. The light was on, and the door was ajar. Henry screamed and ran inside. Susan put up her hand, preventing Mike from stepping into a puddle of blood. She approached the desk, wincing as she moved her sticky feet. All she could see was the back of the woman, her auburn hair matted with blood, slumped over in the desk chair, facing the window.

"Oh God, Emily!" screamed Susan.

Susan held her breath. She put her hand on Mike's shoulder as they waited for the seconds to pass. Henry, breathing hard, swung the chair around.

Please let her be alive. Susan trembled. *Not another murder. Not Emily.*

Henry bent down. "It's not her. Thank God it isn't her." He felt for a pulse. "She's dead."

"Who?" said Susan. "If that's not Emily, then who is it?"

"Henry, holding on to the chair for support, said, "It's Emily's colleague, Martha Peterson."

"She looks just like Emily," said Susan, brushing her hand on the woman's cheek.

"Hey, try not to touch things. We don't want to mess up the crime scene," said Mike.

She rolled her eyes at him as if to say, *You really think I don't know that?*

Henry addressed Susan's comment. "Yes, students asked Emily all the time if they were sisters. Same reddish hair, same length. About the same age and build too. My God, Martha is dead!"

Mike dialed 911. Susan noticed a gash on the back of Martha's head. "It looks like someone snuck up behind her and bashed her on the head." Her eyes scanned the room for a murder weapon.

"Poor Martha. Who did this and why?" said Henry.

"I hate to mention it, but this is Emily's office and she was facing away from the door. Do you think…?"

"Susan, you think someone tried to kill Emily?" Henry looked around the office. "You're right. They may have been after Emily." He frantically stuck his head out the door and called into the hallway. "Emily, where are you?"

The campus security guard appeared on the scene. "I heard screaming." He walked over to the body. "Is she dead?"

"Yes, and my wife is missing. Did you pass anyone in the parking lot?" asked Henry.

"No, no one. It's always pretty deserted here at night." He called the local police.

"I'll check the ladies' room," said Mike. "We passed it coming in."

Susan noticed a purse on the floor beside the desk. "Henry, is that Martha's purse?"

"No, that's Emily's." Henry spoke in a high-pitched voice as he rummaged through the purse. "Wallet, brush, lipstick… Her keys aren't in here!" He looked out the window. "And her car isn't in the parking lot. She parks behind the building."

Sirens blared, and the EMTs rushed in followed by two young police detectives.

"I'm Detective Ron Wooster. This is my partner, Megan O'Leary. Let's clear the room and let the paramedics work." Megan secured the room with crime tape and snapped photos from every angle. Detective

Wooster sent the security guard to check the rest of the building.

"I think whoever did this was after my wife." Henry's face was flushed. "And she's missing. My wife. Her purse is here, but she's gone."

"His wife is Emily. She looks just like the victim," said Susan.

"Do you know the victim?" asked Detective Wooster.

"Not personally. Her name is Martha Peterson."

"She's my wife's colleague," said Henry. "Her office is down the hall."

The detective pulled out a legal pad and started writing. "Start from the beginning."

Susan said, "We came from New York to visit our friends here, Henry and Emily Fox. When we got to their cabin, no one was home until Henry came in."

Henry continued. "Emily didn't answer the phone, so I... I came here. She was supposed to be done teaching hours ago. My God, Emily. I still don't know if she's safe. I have to find her." He pulled out his phone to call. "It goes straight to voice mail."

The medical examiner arrived at the scene. Detective Wooster asked Henry to show him Martha's office. Inside, Susan spotted a purse on Martha's desk, which the detective opened. He checked the wallet. "It belongs to Martha Peterson."

Detective Wooster's partner found them. "She's only been dead an hour or so. The medical examiner says it looks like blunt force trauma. They're taking the body in now."

Mike said, "Do you think it was a robbery?"

"No," said Detective Wooster. "We checked the purse. Wallet's in there with a couple of twenties. Credit cards are there. The victim is still wearing a gold necklace and wedding ring."

"Wedding ring?" said Susan. Her heart fell, thinking about Martha's husband hearing the news.

"She's a widow," said Henry. "I think she has a sister out in California. Detective, I have to find my wife. Can you put out an alert?"

"Why don't you check at home?"

"The cell service wasn't working when I was at the house," said Susan.

"Yeah, it's spotty at best. What if she isn't there?" Henry wrung his hands together.

"Let's go see," said Mike. "I'll drive."

"Call me and let me know if she doesn't turn up," said Detective Wooster.

Susan, Mike, and Henry piled into the car and sped toward Maplewood. On their way, they heard sirens. The road was blocked with emergency vehicles.

"That's Lake Pleasant. Looks like a car ran off the road. It's sticking half out of the lake." Henry parked, and they ran to the side of the lake where a crane was being hooked up to a car. Henry was frantic. "What if…" He looked around. "And who's that in the wet suit? A diver? Is someone down there? Is my wife down there?"

Mike said, "Calm down. We don't know if it's Emily."

"That's Emily's car! Oh God. It's her car."

"Are you sure?"

"Of course I am. If Emily's… If she's…"

Mike led him to a tree stump. "Sit down. We'll talk to the paramedics as soon as the car is out."

Susan pulled her coat tightly around her and tried to get a closer look before being shooed away by a fireman. She could hear the ice cracking above the grinding of the crane and for a moment felt as though she was going to pass out. The sun had set hours ago, but the lights from the emergency vehicles lit the scene like a late winter photo shoot.

She asked a nearby officer, "What's happening? Is anyone in the car?"

"Ma'am, we're trying to find out."

"But I have to know. My friend is missing." She started toward the lake.

The officer put his hand on her arm. "Look, ma'am. We can work better with a clear field. Please stay back."

"If you let me see, I can tell you who it is." She walked toward the lake. *How long can a person last in freezing cold water? They need to hurry.*

"Lady, let us do our job. Step back. Last thing we need is to have to pull an old lady out of the frozen pond while trying to extricate a car and locate a body."

Did he really just call me an old lady? Susan wished her detective daughter, Lynette, was with her to take charge and keep things moving. She'd keep her informed as to what was happening so she wouldn't feel like a helpless deer staring at headlights. At least she hoped that's what she'd do after realizing her mom could be a valuable asset. After all, who helped solve a principal's murder, cleared a friend from murder charges against a student, and restored the safety of her granddaughter's preschool? That would be her. Old lady indeed.

She walked over to Mike and Henry. The grinding sound grew louder and quicker.

"Look, there's the car. They're pulling it all the way out." Susan started to move toward it, but Mike grabbed her arm.

"Give them a few minutes." He met Susan's eyes and darted his own to Henry. Susan realized he was trying to soften the potential blow to their friend.

Henry stood up. "I have to see if she's in there. What if she's... dead? The lake water is freezing. What if she got knocked out in the accident and couldn't swim out of the car?"

Susan snuck closer and took cover behind a tree so she could hear the conversation between the officers and paramedics.

A uniformed officer said, "The window was shattered, maybe with a hammer. The body is gone. The divers are searching."

Susan stepped out from behind the tree. "Or maybe she escaped from the car and is sitting, freezing, waiting for medical attention. Did you check the area?"

"Lady, please. I told you to stay back. We have it under control," said the officer.

Susan went back to Mike and Henry. "She isn't in the car, and the window is smashed."

"Smashed? She had one of those tools to break the window in just this type of situation. Emily is smart. I'll bet she smashed the window herself and swam to the surface. She's an excellent swimmer."

Susan's heart twisted in her chest. She couldn't imagine losing her friend, and even worse, couldn't imagine Henry losing his wife, just when they had so much to look forward to here in their new town. She turned around and gasped. Henry screamed. Mike said, "Is it possible?"

Standing under a tree, wrapped in a blanket, was Emily. She was accompanied by an older woman in a parka.

"Oh my God. Emily! You're alive!" Henry ran to her and hugged her tight. "Are you okay? I was so scared that... You're trembling. Let the paramedics look at you."

"I can't stop shaking. Martha. She's dead. I went to the ladies' room and came back. There was blood. Blood on the floor. Blood on her head."

"Are you hurt? You're soaking wet. How'd you get out of the car?"

"I'm okay. I broke the window and swam out. *He* was after me. He must have killed Martha."

Henry addressed the woman in the parka. "Coralee, how did you find her?"

"I went out to call the dog back in, and I saw Emily walking toward me. I brought her inside, and we were about to call the police. I heard sirens, so we figured they'd found the car."

"Or the monster who killed Martha and tried to kill me," said Emily.

Detective Wooster ran over to them. "Mrs. Fox, are you okay? Had you remained in the car, you'd never have survived. You saved your own life. Let the paramedics look at you."

"It's okay. I'm not hurt, just cold and shaken up."

"Can I ask you some questions?"

Coralee owned a bed-and-breakfast in the community. She said, "My inn is right there. Can you question her inside where it's warm? I'll make us some tea."

Detective Wooster hesitated for a moment, then agreed. "I'll let the team know you're safe, and I'll be right over."

Chapter 2

Coralee's place, The Sugarbury Outside Inn, was a fixture in Sugarbury Falls. It was painted yellow with white shutters, and a porch surrounded the first floor. Guests drove up to enjoy long romantic weekends, to tour St. Edwards College with their high school students, to enjoy the outdoor activities, and to celebrate milestones like anniversaries and birthdays. The inn was famous for its weekend brunch and home-cooked dinners. Coralee led Susan, Mike, Emily, and Henry up the trail to the inn.

"This looks like a gingerbread house straight out of a fairy tale," said Susan, trying to break the tension. She stepped onto the front porch.

"Unless you think I'm going to fatten you all up and throw you into an oven, I'll take that as a compliment," said Coralee.

Once inside, Coralee took them through a sitting area where a fire crackled in the fieldstone fireplace. Several sweater-clad guests gathered near the hearth, sipping from mugs and munching on brownies.

"Let's go back there where it's more private," said Coralee. She handed Emily an afghan. "I'm going to make us some hot chocolate. I'll be right back."

"Are you feeling any warmer?" asked Susan.

Emily answered, "I'm still shivering, but I think it's more from the sight of Martha in that chair than from being drenched."

Detective Wooster rang the bell on the lobby counter.

"We're back here," said Henry. "In the alcove."

Coralee returned from the kitchen with mugs of hot chocolate and a plate of cookies.

"Mrs. Fox, start at the beginning. Tell me everything that happened today."

"I… I taught my class this morning. Afterward, Martha, my colleague, asked if she could show me a paper she was working on for publication. We went into my office. Spent quite a bit of time discussing her paper."

"Martha was a teacher?" asked Detective Wooster.

"Yes, an assistant professor in English. She taught creative writing too—and she co-ordinated the the basic English comp course."

"Go on. Did you see or hear anyone enter the building?"

"No, we were wrapped up in our work. I had to use the restroom. Martha was sitting in my chair; I'd been reclining on the sofa under the window. My back aches if I sit in that chair too long."

"You went out for how long? Five minutes maybe?"

"More like ten. I heard someone in the hall, but by the time I came out, no one was there. I went back to my office and saw blood on the floor. I felt my heart beating like a metronome set for a Sousa march. Then I saw the wound on Martha's head. I screamed, then took a few deep breaths to get my head on straight and felt for a pulse."

The front door slammed shut, and Coralee yelled to a young man about to climb the stairway. "Noah, come here. I was getting worried. You were supposed to be home hours ago. I left your dinner warming in the oven."

The young man, mid-twenties, was dressed in black from his boots to his parka. He wore heavy gloves and a ski cap.

"Susan, Mike, Detective, this is my son Noah."

"How do you do." Noah took off his glove to shake their hands. That's when Susan noticed his bruised fingers and spatters of blood on the back of his hand. "I'm going upstairs to shower before dinner."

Come on, Susan said to herself. *Blood? Bruises? Maybe he'd been painting. Or maybe I'm imagining things. I'm awfully tired.*

Noah left, and Detective Wooster resumed his questioning.

"Mrs. Fox, were you able to detect a pulse?"

"I couldn't tell. I heard a noise. I was afraid the intruder was still in the building, so I grabbed my keys from the top of my desk and ran out to the parking lot. I realized I'd left my purse and couldn't call 911, so I sped along, trying to get some help."

"You were speeding. Is that how you wound up in the lake?"

"Oh, no. It wasn't because I was speeding. I was being followed. I saw headlights in the rearview mirror. Then I felt the truck crash into me. He didn't stop pushing my car until it landed in the lake." Henry squeezed her hand. "The front of my car was sinking fast. I knew I couldn't open the door until the pressure equalized. I remembered the tool I'd bought after seeing a segment on *The Doctor Oz Show*. I used it to smash the glass, and I swam out."

"That's my wife. Levelheaded and smart under the worst possible pressure. Thank God you made it out." He squeezed her hand again.

Susan noticed Emily was still shivering. "Coralee, do you maybe have a pair of sweats or something dry for Emily to change into?"

"Sure, I should have thought of that earlier." The bell at the front desk rang just as she got up to find clothes.

Susan said, "Go to your guest. I'll get it."

"My room's at the top of the stairs. Bottom dresser drawer."

Susan climbed the steps, wincing at the creaking sound her knees sometimes made these days. She pushed open the door at the top of the steps and walked into a pale blue room with a four-poster bed. She heard the shower running. *This must be the wrong room. It must be her son's.* She noticed a bulging knapsack on the bed with one wet strap. *Is that water, or is it blood? Come on, Susan. Everything isn't a mystery to solve. You came here to visit your friends.*

Just then the water stopped running, and Susan darted across the hall where she found Coralee's room, retrieved the dry sweats, and went back to her friends.

"Coralee, how old is your son?" asked Susan.

"He's twenty-six. He takes classes at St. Edwards and helps me out here at the inn. In the winter, he makes extra money giving cross-country ski lessons to the guests."

Emily changed into the dry clothes, and the detective resumed his questioning.

"Mrs. Fox, did the assailant see you?"

"I don't know. He obviously followed me to my car and ran me into the lake. I suppose he was worried I'd seen him."

"Did you see him?"

"No. I scrambled out of the building after I saw what had happened. I can't even tell you what kind of truck he was driving. I was so upset after seeing Martha." Emily wiped tears with the sleeve of the sweatshirt.

"It's okay, Mrs. Fox. I'll try to wrap this up so you can go home and get some rest. Do you have any idea who may have wanted either you or Martha Peterson dead?"

"Wanted *us* dead? No, of course not."

Detective Wooster handed her a card. "We'll talk again soon. I'll have a patrol car outside your house tonight. Just in case."

The detective left. Emily said, "What does he mean by *just in case*? Am I in danger?"

Henry put his arm around her. "It's better to be safe than sorry. I'm sure the killer will get as far away from here as possible. He's probably across the Canadian border by now."

Chapter 3

Susan slept soundly, curled under a quilt next to Mike in Emily and Henry's guest room. The white wrought iron bed matched the nightstands on either side. Mike was lying awake, staring at the ceiling.

"Mike, are you okay? Did you sleep well?"

"Yeah. I'm just trying to figure out who would want to hurt Emily. She doesn't have a mean bone in her body. And even if she did, they haven't been living here long. I doubt she's had time to make enemies."

"There's still the possibility that the killer was after Martha Peterson."

"But he ran Emily's car into the lake. Either he realized he'd missed his target…"

"Or he was afraid Emily could identify him."

Henry knocked on the door. "Breakfast is ready. I'm sure you must be hungry after last night's excitement."

Susan pulled on a flannel robe. She and Mike followed Henry into the kitchen.

"Ah, coffee. It smells hot and strong. Just what I need."

Mike said, "And are these cinnamon buns?" He reached for one, and Susan grabbed his wrist.

"Just one. No more heart attacks for you. Remember what happened when you let up on your diet the last time we traveled."

"You mean in Atlanta? It was just indigestion. No harm, no foul."

Henry pulled a carton of eggs from the refrigerator. "Fried or scrambled?"

"We'll take scrambled. Do you have any of that nonstick spray?" Mike rolled his eyes at his wife.

Emily, yawning, came into the kitchen. "Henry, are you taking care of our guests?"

"I was just about to start some eggs. Grab some coffee and sit down."

Susan and Mike joined Emily at the farm-style table with the tiled top. A long bench provided seating against the kitchen wall while wooden chairs faced across the other side of the table. A rooster-shaped kitchen clock over the table read eight o'clock.

Susan poured creamer into her mug of coffee. "Emily, were you able to get any sleep?"

"Hardly. The image of Martha slumped over in my chair, me screaming, the blood on the floor…"

Susan hugged her. "I know. It will haunt you for a while. At least you're safe. I'm surprised no one else on the floor came out when they heard you scream."

"Normally someone would have. The new college president was inaugurated yesterday afternoon. It was a huge deal. Classes were canceled, and virtually all faculty and staff were in attendance. I wanted to come home and get ready for your visit instead. As I was leaving, Martha came into my office. She wanted my opinion on a paper she was working on."

"You didn't hear anyone in the hall?"

"No. I went to the ladies' room, and when I came back… You know the rest."

Henry set a bowl of eggs on the table. "Dig in. I was thinking after breakfast we can take a tour around the community. Ever been snowshoeing?"

"No," said Mike. "Sounds like fun."

Emily poured orange juice. "That does sound like fun, but there's a bit of a learning curve. How about we take the Jeep now and do some snowshoeing this afternoon? I need to put away some notes for my book, but it can wait. I was thinking we could eat dinner at Coralee's tonight."

"What's your book about?" asked Susan.

"It's a true crime story. This summer marks the ten-year anniversary of the mysterious disappearance of a St. Edwards student, Ashley Young. She was last seen on campus but seemed to vanish into thin air. She was supposed to eat dinner at her parents' house that evening, but she never showed up. Her car was gone from the student parking lot."

"They never found a body?"

"No. Or the car. Word was she took off after breaking up with her abusive boyfriend. Her parents said she'd never leave town without telling them. Besides, she hadn't packed any clothes, and her boxes of contact lenses were still in her bathroom."

"What did the police say?"

"They found no evidence of foul play. There were no witnesses, no body. Ashley was legally an adult. After a while, they stopped looking. Wrote it off as a voluntary disappearance."

Henry said, "Enough talk about crime. Let's take a tour."

After showering and getting dressed, they all hopped into the Jeep.

The sky was ocean blue, and the sun sparkled on the snow. Rolling her window halfway down, Susan took a deep breath and savored the clean, crisp air.

Henry pulled onto the gravel road. "The community is one big circle around the lake. St. Edwards College is off to the right, about a ten-minute drive if the road is clear. We'll go clockwise." Henry continued driving. "That's Kurt Olav's house on the left. You met him the other day. He moved here from Minnesota a dozen years ago."

"Did his family come up with him?" asked Susan.

"He doesn't ever mention a family. He's very tight-lipped, doesn't share a bunch of personal stuff. I figure it's a Minnesota thing." Henry kept driving.

He drove past an abandoned cabin in need of paint. "The owners haven't been up here in years. That's what Coralee tells us. I remember the family who lived there when we spent our summers here growing up. Cabin bustled what with three kids living there. What a shame it's sitting empty."

Susan peeked through the window. "If they ever want to sell, let us know. Mike and I can use a retirement home."

"Sure," said Mike. "Like you'd be willing to move hours away from Annalise, not to mention our daughter and her husband."

"You know my pressure points too well. I could never leave my precious granddaughter." Just picturing Annalise brought a smile to Susan's face. "And now that Jason and Lynette are going to adopt a baby from China, you're right. I couldn't move away from Westbrook."

Emily turned to Susan. "They're adopting a baby? You didn't tell me that. How wonderful. There'll be—What?—A three-year span or so between the baby and Annalise? That's perfect."

"I can't wait," said Susan. "Being a grandparent is the best thing in the world. That's a cute cabin." The small wooden cabin had two rocking chairs on the porch outside the front door. Susan could see bright, gingham curtains hanging from the front window.

Emily turned back to Susan. "Another St. Edwards professor, Morgan Reynolds, in the math department, and her husband live there. She barely speaks to me. Her husband, Gerald, had my job until he was fired last year. I replaced him, which doesn't sit well with Morgan even though I had nothing to do with him losing his job. Gerald is in his late fifties. Had a few more years until retirement. Morgan's quite a bit younger. Rumor is she was his student at his previous job and was let go when they started dating."

"Why did they fire him from St. Edwards?" asked Susan.

"He started acting strange. He blew up at his students randomly for no reason. He missed classes pretty regularly too."

A Jetta passed them, pulling into the opposite lane in order to do so. Henry explained it was the only way to do it on a two-lane road.

"Most of the time no one is in much of a hurry around here," said Henry. "Those two are the exception. Young couple, Kiki and Buzz. When Kiki's mom died, they inherited her place. Want no part of living here. They're what we refer to as city folks."

Emily gave Henry a playful swat. "City folks? Since when did you start talking like you grew up in Alabama rather than Hartford, Connecticut?"

"I'm turning into a regular country bumpkin I guess. Anyhow," Henry continued, "they had jobs in one of those newfangled millennial companies in Manhattan. You know, the kind with nap chairs and treadmill desks."

Mike said, "So what on earth are they doing to make a living in Sugarbury Falls?"

"The company lets them telecommute. Can you imagine? And they're complaining because they want to go back and live in the city. They live next door to us."

"Not exactly neighborly either," said Emily. "There's a company that builds tiny houses—Peewee Miniatures. It's the latest fad, tiny affordable homes. And I do mean *tiny*. Some are even portable. Imagine dragging your house behind you on a trailer. A step up from the old RVs."

"If they're portable, why do they need your land?"

"Not all are portable. Peewee envisions a whole tiny community! The owner wants to include a tiny general store and a tiny post office—even a tiny barbershop/hair salon. Idiotic if you ask me."

"Don't you already have those things here?" asked Susan.

"Yes, but it's a bit of a ride, especially when the roads are bad. This community would have everything within walking distance. He's even planning tiny bungalow rentals, which would threaten Coralee's place."

"A newfangled type of vacation. Like staying in one of those ice hotels or something."

"Would make for some cool pictures to post on Facebook," said Henry. "Right, Susan? Wouldn't you hit *Like* if you saw that status?" Henry's tone was full of his famous sarcasm.

Emily continued. "They want to buy up both places——theirs and ours—so they can build on the land. We're not willing to sell, but Kiki and Buzz are dying to. They hate us for keeping them up here in paradise when they could be fighting pollution and traffic back in the city."

"Got to be the most spoiled generation ever," said Mike.

Susan shielded her eyes from the glare bouncing off the snow. "Isn't that the inn we were at last night?"

"Yes, it is. We'll come back for dinner tonight if that's okay with you both."

"Of course it is," Susan added. "After a day of learning to snowshoe, we'll be ready for a relaxing dinner. I heard snowshoeing burns tons of calories."

Emily said, "At least enough to negate a piece of Coralee's apple strudel."

Chapter 4

Several inches of fresh snow blanketed Emily and Henry's yard. Henry gathered up snowshoes for all four of them, having borrowed two pair from Coralee's inn. Coralee offered complimentary recreational equipment to her guests and had plenty of extras that she happily lent to residents when they entertained guests.

"That snow last night gives us something to work with," said Henry. He helped Susan and Mike strap on the snowshoes. "Go slowly. It's a little tricky at first."

"No problem," said Susan. She struggled to keep her balance. Mike took to them easily. Suspicious, she asked, "Are you sure you never did this before?"

"Not in this lifetime," said Mike.

A weathered barn was between the Fox cabin and Kurt Olav's place. Susan felt as if she could have crawled to it faster than she was snowshoeing toward it. The wind blew snow over her boots as she plodded along out of breath.

"Henry, don't you think you should take a look at the barn door while we're out here?" said Emily. "Remember, Kurt said it was open the other day."

Henry led the group to the barn and put his gloved hand over the door. "It's closed as securely as ever. Maybe Kurt just thought it was open."

"Kurt has quite the eyes for details. I doubt he was wrong," said Emily.

Henry took off his glove and tugged at the door. Then he opened it and examined the latch. "Nothing broken here."

"What do you use the barn for?" asked Susan. "Do you plan on getting animals?"

"As much as I love horses, Henry is right. They are too much work. I haven't been in the barn since we moved here. Maybe someday I'll turn it into a writing studio."

"Or a woodworking shop," added Henry.

Turning around was harder than it looked. Susan toppled over into the snow. While she was on the ground, she saw something shiny in the snow. Brushing it off with her glove, she picked up a gold button. Henry bent down to help her up.

"What've you got there?"

"It's a button. Looks like it came off a coat. Is it yours?"

"Not mine. Both Emily and I favor zippered parkas. I don't recognize it."

They continued, progressing slowly toward the lake. Susan whipped around when she heard the sound of a snowmobile. A young couple on an old-fashioned two-seater whizzed past, then turned around and parked in front of them. The woman had long dark hair that tumbled out of her knit cap. The young man wore a heavy-duty leather jacket. Henry introduced them.

"Susan and Mike, these are our neighbors, Kiki and Buzz Montaldo. Kiki and Buzz, these are our dear friends from back in Westbrook."

"Kiki and Buzz also used to live in New York. They worked in Manhattan." Emily winked at Susan as if to remind her about the discussion they'd had previously regarding millennials.

"Must miss your friends. It's hard to make new ones once you hit a certain age," said Buzz. He turned to Susan. "Maybe you can convince your friends to move back home with you. This cold weather is hard on your health. The elderly can be wiped out by a simple flu.

Immune systems aren't what they were when you were younger."

"Our immune systems are in top shape, but we appreciate your concern. We've both got a lot of years ahead of us," said Emily. "You won't convince us to sell our place."

Buzz said, "You two are crazy old goats. How can you pass up the money Peewee is offering to buy your house? We could both sell, make a hefty profit, and move back to civilization."

"As long as you two hold out, Peewee won't buy our place. They need both lots in order to build the Tiny House community they envision," Kiki continued. "You'd have enough to rent a cabin up here *and* get yourselves a nice place back home."

"It's not about the money," said Emily.

Henry said, "We need to be getting back. See you two around."

Susan heard Buzz mumble "selfish goats" under his breath before starting up the snowmobile and speeding away.

"What was that all about?" said Susan.

"They're trying to bully us into selling," said Henry. "A fruitless endeavor, but if they want to keep hitting a brick wall, let them scrape up their knuckles."

Chapter 5

Susan dragged her weary body into the shower. A bruise was developing on the heel of her hand where she'd tried to break her fall earlier. The scraped skin burned when the water hit it, but all in all, the shower was restorative. She was ready for a cozy dinner at the inn.

Mike knocked on the bathroom door. "Come on; they made a reservation for six o'clock. And I need to jump in the shower too."

Susan wrapped herself in the fluffy guest towel and came out, freezing in spite of the stuffy heat pouring from the radiator. She gave Mike a playful flash, opening and closing the towel.

"Hmm. Now you're trying to make us late." He wrapped his arms around her and gave her an enthusiastic kiss. "Later, beautiful."

After nearly forty years together, Mike always erases my stretch marks and wrinkles from my self-image. I'm the luckiest lady in the world, getting my confidence boosted by my own personal cheerleader every time I start to fret about my aging body.

Henry knocked on the guest room door. "Are you about ready? The inn fills up on a Saturday night. We don't want to lose our reservation."

"We'll be out in a minute," said Susan. She pulled on black pants and a teal sweater, which everyone said made her eyes pop from behind her bifocals.

Henry parked the Jeep in front of the inn just at the stroke of six. Most tables were already full when Coralee greeted them at the door.

"I'm so glad you came tonight. I made my famous apple strudel for dessert. Emily, are you doing okay? Have the police gotten any leads about Martha's murder?"

"We haven't heard anything yet. I hope they catch whoever did this and lock him away for life."

The dining area glowed with table candles and strategically placed tea lights. A golden orange log crackled in the fireplace.

"This has to be the coziest restaurant I've ever been to," said Susan. She could smell the fresh-baked bread when a waiter carrying a napkin-covered straw basket brushed past her.

"I'll take that as a compliment." Coralee showed them to a table in front of lattice-paned double doors. Soft floodlights washed the patio in a pink glow. In summer months, diners often opted to eat al fresco while overlooking a small golf course.

"Oh no," said Emily. "Look, there's Morgan and her husband Gerald. She's the professor who thinks I took her husband's job. Such a sourpuss always. I'm surprised to see them out of the house. Mostly they live like hermits. Watch. She won't say *hello* when they pass us."

Morgan looked like a hippie-era holdout. A paisley, floor-length caftan peeked out from under her faded denim coat. Susan imagined her frizzy, shoulder-length curls adorned with a crown of daisies, but instead, Morgan wore a knitted cap, which tied under the chin like a baby bonnet. gypsy-like gold hoops hung from her ears, completing the ensemble.

Susan whispered to Emily, "She's a great candidate for *Ambush Makeover*."

Emily giggled. "Too bad that show, *What Not to Wear*, isn't still on TLC. Stacy and Clinton would have a field day."

"Come on, ladies. I thought you both graduated from high school already," said Henry.

Coralee led Morgan and Gerald toward their seats, pausing when they passed Emily and Henry's table.

Emily said, "Hello, Morgan and Gerald. Nice to see you two out and about on a Saturday night. These are our friends, Susan and Mike Wiles, from New York."

Gerald grunted and shook their hands. Susan, looking at his balding gray hair and slumped posture, guessed he was in his sixties.

"Nice to meet you," said Morgan. "Is your friend looking for a college teaching position too? Should I be worried?"

"Come on, Morgan. I'd never even heard of St. Edwards until *after* Gerald's position was advertised. I wish you could get past that."

Henry said, "I saw the president's inauguration ceremony on TV. Looked like the whole university and most of the town was there. Did you go?"

"We were there from start to finish. It was lovely," said Morgan. "Now, excuse us. I'm getting hungry."

Coralee sat them at the next table. Susan had a direct view of both Morgan and her husband throughout the meal.

"You have to try the corn chowder," said Emily.

"And the maple-crusted chicken breast is out of this world," added Henry.

Following their friend's suggestions, Mike and Susan ordered. Then the waiter went to Morgan and Gerald's table.

"Guys, look," Susan whispered, discreetly pointing. "Why is Gerald pulling out his credit card? They haven't even ordered yet."

Henry grabbed a hot roll from the basket. "The man's a little off. I can't imagine him teaching."

"Morgan is holding his wrist. She must be telling him to put it away," said Emily. "Ah, here's our soup. Let's eat."

As Susan was eating, she noticed Coralee's son, Noah, tiptoeing past the front desk and up the stairs which Susan knew led to his room. He was dressed all in black and carried the same backpack she'd seen in his room the other night. *Why is he sneaking around in his own place? And what's with the funeral garb? Young man on a Saturday night. Surely not date attire.*

"How's the chicken?"

Mike swallowed and said, "Henry, this is amazing."

"And it's heart healthy to boot," said Susan. "Baked, not fried."

Mike gave her that familiar "stop being the food police" look.

"Are you feeling okay since your heart attack?" said Emily.

"Just fine. I've lost a few pounds, and I take walks almost daily. This heart will be ticking for many a moon."

At the next table, Gerald stood up and put his napkin on his plate. Morgan stood up too, put her hands on his shoulders, and sat him back down. Then she whispered something in his ear. They didn't appear to be arguing. *Morgan is very gentle when she touches him,* Susan thought. *I wonder if he's ill.*

Her thoughts were interrupted when a screaming woman in a cocktail dress entered the dining room, running up to Coralee.

"It's gone! My diamond necklace is gone. I left it on the dresser while I took a shower. I came out, and it wasn't there. We were getting ready for the alumni reunion at St. Edwards. As it is, we're going to miss it."

Coralee spoke softly. "Calm down. Are you sure it's gone? Did you look under the bed? Maybe it fell behind the dresser."

"No, no. I'm positive it's gone. It belonged to my mother. It was there before my shower. Look, ask my husband."

A handsome man in a tailored suit stepped into the dining room. "I called the police. They want us to come down to the station and file a report. I already called Uber."

Uber? Susan wondered. *Car service up here in wilderness country? Who would have thought? I'll bet it makes Kiki and Buzz feel more at home.*

Coralee escorted the upset guests to the lobby.

"A robbery here at the inn? Does that happen often?" asked Susan.

Emily said, "Not that I've heard of."

Henry said, "It's a safe little community, perhaps too safe. People don't even lock their doors around here. False sense of security."

Coralee returned to the dining room and chatted with the diners, going from table to table.

"That Coralee has a knack for this," said Susan. "I'm sure she's upset about the robbery, yet she comes right back in with a smile on her face and a heaping dose of hospitality."

Coralee walked over to their table.

Emily said, "Coralee, are you okay?"

Coralee said, "I'm sincerely hoping she just misplaced the necklace. Looks like you enjoyed your dinner!"

"I'd have licked the plate if it wouldn't have embarrassed my tablemates," said Mike.

"I hope you saved room for dessert. Hot apple strudel with homemade vanilla bean ice cream."

"We're in," said Henry.

"Coralee, have you had any other problems with theft lately? Must be hard with strangers coming in and out. Who knows if you can trust all of them?"

"For years I haven't had one instance of robbery. In the past few months, this is the third time. One guest had jewelry stolen while she and her husband were out on the slopes. They swear their door was locked. Another guest had cash missing from his wallet. I tell every guest we have a safe to lock away valuables, but no one ever takes me up on the offer."

Henry said, "Unless you've had a guest who has been here that long, it has to be someone who lives in town."

"Kiki and Buzz Montaldo are the only newcomers other than yourselves. I'll remind the guests to lock their doors and take advantage of the safe. If it gets out that we have theft problems, it will kill my business."

When every last crumb of dessert had been eaten, the foursome pushed away from the table and stepped into the lobby. The door opened, and Coralee's son, Noah, walked in. This time, he was dressed in a nice pair of dark-wash jeans, a red pullover sweater, and a wool coat. Coralee stepped into the lobby when she saw her son.

"Noah, did you have fun on your date tonight?" asked Coralee. She turned to Susan and Mike. "You remember my son, Noah, from the other night. He just got back from a hot date."

"Yes, of course. Nice to see you again," said Mike.

Susan said, "I remember. So where do guys take dates in this town if it isn't here to eat at the inn?"

Noah fumbled. "We, um, went out for a night hike along the lake."

"Pretty cold out there, isn't it?" said Susan.

"That's the point, right, Noah?" Mike gave him a high five.

Why is Noah lying? Susan wondered. *I know I saw him sneak in wearing black less than an hour ago. Unless he has a twin, it's impossible that he just now came home.*

Henry pulled his keys from his coat pocket. "Ready to go? Coralee, thanks for yet another wonderful meal."

Chapter 6

"Shh, Mike. They'll hear us," said Susan. Mike was grabbing her under the quilt in the white wrought iron bed.

"Their bedroom is all the way upstairs in the loft. No one but the cat will hear us, and he's not talking. Besides, exercise is good for my heart."

"Well, if you put it like that..." She began kissing him.

"Knock, knock. Breakfast is ready," said Henry.

Susan whispered, "See."

"To be resumed later," she whispered to her husband, then louder, "Henry, we'll be right out."

Emily was mixing pancake batter with fresh blueberries when they walked into the kitchen. Susan breathed in the coffee aroma.

"Grab a mug. It's freshly ground vanilla coffee," said Emily. "Sugar and creamer are already on the table."

"Local maple syrup too," said Henry. "Wait till you try it."

The pancakes melted in Susan's mouth. She hoped they couldn't tell she was drooling over them. Mike ate with gusto.

"Susan, I was going to drop by the college this morning. The police said they're finished working the crime scene, and I want to straighten up my office before classes resume tomorrow. Want a tour of the campus?"

"I'd love it."

"Mike and I will meet you over there," said Henry.

Emily grabbed her briefcase and took Susan over to her office. They parked in front of Emily's office building.

"Let's go," said Susan. Emily was still grasping the steering wheel. "Are you okay? We don't have to go in today. Let's turn around and visit some antique stores or something."

"No, I'll be okay." She took a deep breath. "I want to get this over with. I have to teach a class tomorrow, so I'd better get a grip now."

Susan grabbed Emily's elbow, and together they went into the building. Emily searched in her purse, took out her keys, and dropped them before she could unlock the door.

"I'm such a klutz."

Susan noticed Emily's hands trembling. "I'll get them." When she reached down to pick up the keys, she saw an earring caught under the door. "Emily, is this yours?"

"No. That's a bit too over-the-top artsy for my taste." The earring had a feather on the end and colored beads strung through the wire.

Inside, the blood puddle had dried on the floor, and the office looked as though it had been ransacked. Emily's hand tremble now swept over her entire body.

"Let's go home," said Susan. "We can call someone to clean this up now that the police are done here."

A balding, middle-aged gentleman in a blue pea coat walked into the office.

"Emily, are you okay?"

"Yes, Joe. I will be."

"I still can't believe Martha is dead. Everyone loved her. I just don't get who would do such a thing."

"Me neither."

Susan said, "They were probably after Emily. It is her office, and she and Martha sort of look alike from the back. She has to be careful. The killer might try again."

"I hadn't thought of that," said the man. "Don't worry. I've got her back."

"Susan, this is Joe Sommers. He's a colleague of mine, becoming a fast friend."

"Nice to meet you, Susan. I've been here at St. Edwards a dozen years already, so I've been showing Emily the ropes."

"He's been a great help getting me oriented. Joe, how was the inauguration ceremony?"

"A little long but fine. Lots of pomp and circumstance, promises for the future, words of inspiration—you know the routine. Thing is, I feel guilty."

"Why?" asked Emily.

"If I'd stayed here in my office, I could have helped you. Maybe I'd have heard the intruder, or if the floor hadn't been deserted, maybe the killer would have turned around and left."

"I appreciate the sentiment, but let go of that. There's nothing you should have done differently. If I had gone to the ceremony… If Martha hadn't asked me to look over her paper…"

"You can't live life with what ifs," said Susan.

Joe gave Emily a hug. "Anything you need, you know I'm here. Nice to meet you Susan."

After Joe left, Susan said, "He seems like a nice man. Is he from Vermont?"

"No, I think he said he grew up in Ohio. He worked at a small college in Columbus before coming here." Emily picked up items from the floor and began straightening up her desk.

"We need bleach to get this blood up. Is there a custodian around?"

"Yes, his office is at the end of the hall."

Susan found the supplies she needed and returned to Emily's office, where her friend was frantically searching through her filing cabinet drawers. Folders were strewn across the floor.

"Emily, what's wrong?"

"My tapes! I have hours' worth of audiotapes I'm using for my book. I kept them in here, and now they're gone."

"Maybe the police moved them when they were working the crime scene."

"I doubt it. The filing cabinet hadn't been disturbed. All the drawers were shut last time I was in here. I had interview recordings with people who knew Ashley Young, people who saw her on campus before she disappeared, her parents. Now they're gone. Hours' worth of work."

"Who would want to steal them? Do you think it was a student who thought the tapes contained test questions?"

"No, they were clearly labeled."

Just then, Detective Wooster knocked on the partially open door. "Sorry to disturb you. Your husband said I could find you here."

"Detective, I just discovered some audiotapes are missing from my filing cabinet. Did the police take them for evidence?"

"No, ma'am. We didn't actually remove items, just took samples and photos."

Susan remembered the earring. "Detective, I found this stuck under the door when we came in this morning." She handed the earring to the detective, who shrugged his shoulders and sealed it in a small baggie.

"Did you find out who killed Martha?" asked Emily.

"Not yet, but we will. Can you tell me who normally has offices on his floor?"

"Me, of course. And Martha did. Also Joe Sommers, my colleague. Erica Satz is on this floor, but she's away on sabbatical this semester. The custodian has his office at the end of the hall. There are some adjunct instructors who share an office."

"How many?"

"I'm not sure. Maybe four or five. They all teach basic English comp. Martha was the coordinator."

"Were any of them around the day Martha was killed?"

"I vaguely remember one of them in Martha's office arguing about something—I think course-related."

"So this adjunct was angry at Martha Peterson, and she was in the building at the time of the murder."

"She was angry, but she stormed out of the building right before Martha came into my office."

"Did you see or hear her drive away?"

"No, but I wasn't listening for that."

"What about Joe Sommers? Did you see him that day?"

"He was here, but then he left to go to the inauguration. Practically everyone who was on campus went to it. Except for me and Martha."

"Is there anyone on campus who would have an ax to grind with you or with Martha?"

Without hesitation, Emily said, "Morgan Reynolds. She's a math professor. Her husband used to have my job, but he was let go for incompetence. She thinks I had something to do with it even though I was hired months after he was fired."

Susan took the scrub brush and poured bleach on the bloodstain. *I might as well try to get this out. It will be much more upsetting for Emily if it remains.*

"So on campus, one of the adjunct instructors was angry with Martha, and this Morgan Reynolds was angry with you."

"Yes, but I can't imagine either as a killer."

"Killers come in all shapes and sizes. You never know. What about enemies from outside of school?"

"No, no one."

Susan interrupted. "What about Buzz and Kiki? They want you to sell your place to Peewee Miniatures so they will buy their place too. They say it will make you both rich."

"They're just a couple of spoiled millennials. If they are on the list, you'd have to add the owner of Peewee also. He's putting on the pressure big time."

Detective Wooster had been jotting notes. "So we'll check this adjunct instructor... What's her name?"

"Sarah Kimberly."

"Sarah Kimberly. Morgan Reynolds, Kiki and Buzz..."

"Montaldo. Their last name is Montaldo."

"Kiki and Buzz Montaldo, and the owner of Peewee Miniatures..."

"Peter Taglieri."

"Sarah Kimberly, Morgan Reynolds, Kiki and Buzz Montaldo, and Peter Taglieri of Peewee Miniatures. Anyone else?"

"Not that I can think of."

"Okay then. We'll be in touch."

Chapter 7

"Sorry we never got around to that tour," said Emily.

Henry chopped onions on the butcher-block cutting board while Emily peeled potatoes.

Mike clumsily peeled and sliced a bunch of carrots. "Another day. It's more important that Emily gets time to relax."

"And cooking does that for me," said Emily. "Susan, you never told me what happened with the Richard Stirling case. Did he get his new trial?"

"He did. After we found who really killed Richard's wife, thirty years later he was released from prison."

"Wow, poor man. Thirty years in jail for a crime he didn't commit."

"Don't feel too sorry for him. He may not be a murderer, but he's a first-class schmuck. He moved in with Audrey, my birth mother, down in Banyan Beach, Florida. He doesn't have a job—after all, who's going to hire a guy in his late seventies with no recent employment experience?"

"And a prison record to boot," added Mike. "He was found innocent, but you know, the fact that he spent the last thirty years in jail is hard to dismiss."

Emily dumped the carrots and onions into the stew pot. Susan added the chicken she'd been cutting.

"Good thing my half brother, George, is looking out for her. Otherwise Richard would be bleeding her dry. She'd already spent a small fortune on his defense. George works for the DEA and has good detective skills."

"It must run in the family," said Emily. "Speaking of mothers, mine is on the prowl for a third husband. She's infiltrated the local Parents Without Partners group even though I'm in my early fifties and my brother is in his late forties. Says it's a great place to find single men."

Henry rinsed his hands in the kitchen sink. "How about a walk while the stew simmers?"

Susan and Mike grabbed their coats. It was a beautiful evening, cold but clear. The sky was full of stars, which seemed especially bright without the interference of city lights. Susan had the Christmas song *Sleigh Ride* running through her head. The song inspired her to grab Mike's hand and snuggle up close as they walked.

A chocolate-black Labrador Retriever leapt into view, followed by Kurt, the neighbor from Minnesota.

"Enjoying a brisk walk I see," said Kurt.

"Working up an appetite for dinner," said Henry.

"Did you ever check out the latch on your barn door? I saw it open again last night."

"Really? I checked, and it seemed to be working fine." He looked over at the barn. "It's shut now."

"And so it is. Hope you don't have a freeloader using your barn for a hotel. Anyhow, I'll keep an eye out. Come on, Prancer." Kurt and his dog disappeared down the road.

Henry said, "As long as we're out here, let me make sure there's no freeloader in there." He pointed at the barn. They all followed on his heels. *Was there an interloper inside?* Susan held her breath while Henry flung open the door. He grabbed a flashlight from the hook on the wall and shone it on each area of the barn as he entered.

"No one's in here. Maybe Kurt's been nipping the Schnapps. There's no sign anyone has tried to break in."

"Let's go home. The stew should be ready by now," said Emily.

The aroma wafted through the front door. Chicken stew with root vegetables. Susan helped Emily whip up some dumplings, and soon they gathered around the table.

"Emily, you sure can cook," said Mike. Susan shot him a look. "You cook almost as well as Susan does." He winked at Emily when Susan turned her head.

"I saw that," said Susan. "Emily, I was wondering, do you think Martha's murder had anything to do with the book you're writing?"

"I was wondering that myself since my tapes were stolen. I can't imagine who would care enough to sabotage the book. Ashley's parents still live in the area. They'd like nothing better than for me to prove foul play was involved. If there was though, the perpetrator surely would have fled the area by now."

"And don't forget, the police think Ashley left of her own free will," added Henry.

"Don't get me started," said Emily. "Through my interviews, I had proof that Ashley never had an abusive boyfriend. That was one theory that encouraged the police to think she left voluntarily."

Changing the subject, Henry suggested having their dessert in the living room. "I heard the news is showing clips from the inauguration tonight."

Emily took out a tin of homemade brownies and set them on the coffee table. Henry turned on the TV.

"Hey, there it is. There's the limo bringing the new president to the auditorium."

Emily said, "What a crowd. Hey, what's that?"

"What?" asked Henry.

"Look, it's the Peewee Miniatures van. And it's driving away from the inauguration. It's the only vehicle heading away," said Henry.

"Interesting. Why was it on campus in the first place?" asked Susan.

Emily said, "You know, if the cold case about Ashley Young resurfaced, it could discourage people from moving into this community. Bad publicity hurts when you're trying to sell houses in what is supposed to be a community where residents don't have to lock their doors."

Susan thought for a moment. "*And* Peewee wants you to sell your property to them so they can build. That's two strikes against you, Emily."

Henry said, "Unless the college plans on building miniature dorms, which I doubt, Peewee has no business being anywhere near the campus."

Chapter 8

The next morning, Emily and Henry took Susan and Mike to brunch at The Outside Inn. As they entered, they passed Detectives Wooster and O'Leary.

"Detective Wooster, any more news about Martha's murder?" asked Henry.

"We narrowed down the murder weapon. It's something like a heavy paperweight or substantial figurine."

"So it could have been used by either a man or a woman?" asked Susan.

"Yes. The weapon was dense enough to kill but not too heavy to lift. We found nothing at the crime scene matching that description, so we believe this was premeditated. The murderer brought the weapon with him. Unless, Mrs. Fox, you noticed anything fitting that description missing from your office."

"No. We were there the other day. Other than my audiotapes, nothing else was taken."

Detective O'Leary said, "There's been more crime in this town in the past few months than there's been in the last decade. Residents are panicking."

"That's not all bad," said Detective Wooster. "We don't want them panicked, but we do want them to be alert and to lock their doors. Stay safe and have a good brunch."

Coralee came into the lobby shaking her head. "Oh dear. Another theft here at the inn. What's going on?"

"Is that why the detectives were here?" asked Emily.

"Yes. Another one of our guests had a necklace stolen. She swears her door was locked and it was taken while she was in the shower, just like the guest who had her necklace stolen last night. Creepy. If it gets out, I'll lose business for sure. And anyway, it makes my skin crawl knowing a prowler has been in my place. I worry about my own safety as well as that of my guests. What with Martha's murder and all. What if the two crimes are related?"

Susan tried to reassure her. "I don't think there's any connection. Martha had jewelry on her when she was killed. Surely a jewel thief would have noticed and taken it."

"I guess that makes sense," said Coralee. "Come on. What kind of hostess am I? Follow me into the dining room. We have fresh blueberry muffins, and the special today is an asparagus omelet with goat cheese. Can I start you with some coffee?"

"Coffee sounds great," said Henry.

Coralee seated them at the same table where they had sat at dinner the other night. Susan craned her neck in an attempt to see what the other diners were eating. Chocolate chip pancakes, eggs, some sort of cooked cereal… *Yum that looks really good. French toast with bananas. That's what I'll have.*

As she eyed the plate of French toast, the man eating it whipped his head around and looked at her. She quickly averted her eyes. She covered the side of her face with her hand, but being Susan, it took only a few seconds before she peeked through her fingers. He was tall and thin, wearing Khakis and a dress shirt. Oh, no! He's getting up and coming over to our table.

"Henry and Emily, enjoying brunch at the inn. You know, if you didn't live here, you could make this a vacation destination and still enjoy Sugarbury Falls without the responsibility that goes along with owning property. You could even vacation with your friends. Who is this handsome couple, Emily?"

"These are our friends, Susan and Mike Wiles. Susan and Mike, this is Peter Taglieri. He owns Peewee Miniatures."

Peter shook their hands. "And where are you from?"

Susan was afraid her face had turned red from the embarrassment of getting caught gawking at Peter Taglieri's French toast. She swallowed and answered, "We're from upstate New York, ninety miles north of the city."

"Then you're within driving distance. I'd love to show you our miniature home models. I have plans for a glorious mini-community—that is, if your friends would stop being so stubborn."

"Give it up," said Henry. "Nothing you say will convince us to sell."

"You're being quite selfish. Think of all the new jobs my project would bring to this town. It's not like the economy couldn't use a boost. Take your friend Coralee. My project would bring in troves of diners and guests. Even that son of hers could benefit. I'm sure I could find a place for him."

"You're wasting your breath."

"You may be able to say no to me, but when the community starts pressuring you, maybe in ways you might not imagine…"

Henry stood up. "Are you threatening us?"

"Of course not. Just giving you some food for thought. Enjoy your brunch."

After he left, Coralee came by. "Was he bothering you?"

"Just the usual," said Emily. "Trying to pressure us to sell, even implying we could face consequences from the community."

"He's blowing hot air. I don't want that man or his business anywhere near here. You keep holding out. I'll see you at Martha's memorial service tomorrow. Her church isn't big enough to accommodate all the expected mourners, so it's being held at the auditorium. Says a lot about how people felt about her."

Stuffed from the delicious meal, the foursome returned to Henry and Emily's cabin.

"We'll need to do some major snowshoeing tomorrow to work off that dinner," said Susan.

"It's vacation," said Emily. "Everyone knows vacation calories don't count."

"At least I left my skinny jeans back home," said Susan. Not that I've been able to wear them in the last decade.

Henry opened the door. "Be careful, everyone. I keep the walk shoveled, but sometimes there are patches of ice."

Susan grabbed Mike's arm and started toward the door behind Emily. Emily pulled a note off the front door.

"What's that?" said Susan.

"I don't know. It was taped to the door." Emily unfolded the note and read it aloud. "Leave it alone, or you'll be sorry."

"Leave what alone?" said Susan.

Henry grabbed the note. "This is a threat. Let's go inside and call the police."

"First a murder in my office. Then my car gets bullied into the lake with me in it. Now this?"

"Don't worry. The police will get to the bottom of it," said Susan.

"Meanwhile," said Henry, "I don't want you going out alone. That goes for you too, Susan."

Chapter 9

The next morning, Henry pulled up in front of the college auditorium. Throngs of people congregated outside.

"Martha was well loved. Look at all these people here for her memorial service," said Emily. "Susan and Mike, you didn't have to come. You didn't even know her, and besides, this is supposed to be a vacation for you."

Susan said, "We're here to support you, and we're not leaving."

The auditorium door opened, and people filed in. Henry led the way. They found seats together in the back row. Susan sat behind a woman wearing a black caftan and long, beaded earrings.

"Emily, is that Morgan Reynolds?" whispered Susan.

"Yes. Remember we ran into them at the inn when we had dinner the other night. She's the one who thinks I took her husband's job. He's right next to her."

Morgan's hair was pulled into a loose ponytail. Susan noticed the oversized earrings Morgan wore. *Where had she seen ones like that recently?*

The new president of St. Edwards walked onto the stage and stood behind the podium.

"Welcome. By the turnout, I am overwhelmed by the number of friends Martha Peterson had in this community. I never had the pleasure of meeting her, but I know her presence will be greatly missed."

The college president continued. He introduced Martha's sister who had flown in from California, then turned the service over to Martha's pastor. Susan looked around the room. She spotted Coralee with her son Noah, and Joe, Emily's friendly coworker. While the pastor spoke, Gerald Reynolds suddenly stood up in the pew in front of Susan.

Susan whispered to Emily, "What's he doing?"

"I don't know. He does weird things like that. Morgan is pulling him back down."

"Do you think he has dementia?"

"It has crossed my mind. Morgan seems to cover his tracks. She's always with him lately."

Susan watched Morgan's earring swing as she turned her head. "Emily! See Morgan's earring?"

"Yes, she wears artsy jewelry all the time."

"That's my point. Remember the earring I found stuck under your office door? The one we gave to the police?"

"It looks like something Morgan would wear. Are you thinking what I'm thinking?"

"That she was in the office when Martha was killed? Do you think she did it?"

Emily folded her hands. "She said she and Gerald were going to the inauguration. Let's tell Detective Wooster our suspicions. I saw him in the back of the auditorium."

"Detectives like to scope out funerals and memorial services to scan for people acting strangely," said Susan. "Lots of times the murderer will be right there at the service."

Henry whispered to her. "Shh. Have some respect. Talk about this later."

The pastor opened the floor for people to share memories of Martha. A student stood up and told a story about the time she was going to drop out, but

Martha Peterson had convinced her to stay. Martha's sister stood up next.

"My sister was my best friend and confidante. She was one of the most loving people this world has ever seen, and I'm not just saying it because I'm her sister. You'll hear the same from her students as well as her boyfriend, who regrettably couldn't be here today."

Susan whispered to Emily, "Boyfriend?"

"She never mentioned a boyfriend to me."

Sarah Kimberly, one of the English Department's adjunct instructors stood up. "Miss Peterson was a competent professor who did her job well." Then she sat down.

"Emily, she doesn't look upset at all. Very businesslike."

"She was angry with Martha over some issue in the basic comp class. I don't know what it was as Martha never mentioned it."

The service concluded with a prayer. The crowd filtered out to the snowy lawn. Susan pointed out the detective. "Let's tell him about the earring."

"Detective, did you find prints on the earring I picked up the other day? I think it belongs to Morgan Reynolds."

"The cleaning crew vacuums every night," said Emily. "It couldn't have been there long."

"We're working on it," said Detective Wooster. "You know we can't discuss an ongoing case."

Susan continued, "You know that Morgan blamed Emily for her husband losing his job. Her husband acts strangely. Maybe he killed Martha and Morgan covered for him."

"We have witnesses who can place Mr. and Mrs. Reynolds at the ceremony during the time of the murder. Let us handle it. We know what we're doing around here."

"Detective, I'm sorry. I didn't mean to imply you didn't. My daughter gets on me all the time for my enthusiasm. She's a detective too."

"Excuse me, I have work to do." He walked over to Martha's sister.

Susan said, "I wonder what he's asking her? Did you know Martha had a boyfriend? And why isn't he here?"

"Martha never mentioned a boyfriend. She never even went on a date as far as I know."

Henry said, "Leave the detective work up to the detectives. There's Coralee. Let's say hello."

Coralee was wearing a black skirt and matching jacket. Noah, in dark jeans and a black coat, accompanied her.

"Coralee, what a nice turnout," said Emily.

"She sure had friends."

"Did you know her well?"

"Yes, she often came to the inn with her boyfriend for dinner."

"Her boyfriend?" Emily and Susan spoke in unison.

"Yes, nice gentleman. Graying hair, nice build. Sometimes they even stayed the weekend. I got the idea he was from out of town. Certainly I'd never seen him around Sugarbury Falls before."

"Why wouldn't he have come to the service if they were that close?" said Emily.

Noah spoke up. "Close? Last time they were at the inn for dinner, they argued very loudly. I even saw him slap Martha's hand. Then Martha stormed out."

"Noah, when was that?" said Emily.

"It was the night before the inauguration."

Susan said, "You mean the night before Martha's murder."

"I hadn't thought of it that way, but yeah."

Flurries fell from the sky. Gray clouds had rolled in, and many of the attendees headed toward their cars.

Joe, Emily's colleague, came over to them. "Lovely service. Martha will be missed. She always had a cheerful smile. Brought me coffee from the general store whenever she stopped there on her way to work."

Emily wiped a tear. "I still don't believe someone wanted to kill her. I'm convinced it was me they were after."

Joe put his arm around her. "I can't imagine anyone wanting to kill you either. Hey, how's your book coming along?"

"I've had a small setback. Someone stole my audiotapes of the witnesses I've been interviewing."

"Really? From your house?"

"No, school. Took them right out of my office."

"What a shame. Did you have them locked up?"

"No, never thought I needed to."

"I've been saying for years those filing cabinets ought to have locks on them."

The wind was picking up, and the sky turned grayer. Morgan and Gerald Reynolds, heads down, walked right past them on the way to the parking lot.

Henry said, "Aren't they the friendliest couple you've ever met?"

"Strange ones," said Joe. "I was sitting by them at the inauguration. They had seats reserved with their programs and coats but didn't walk in until twenty minutes after it started."

"I think Gerald is sick," said Emily. "Maybe Alzheimer's. He never goes anywhere without his wife. It's like she's there to keep him out of trouble."

"You could be right."

A woman wearing a fur coat screamed, "My bracelet. It's gone!"

The man with her yelled, "Police! Aren't there any police here? Call 911."

Detective Wooster stepped forward. "What happened, ma'am?"

"My husband and I came for the service. Our daughter was in Miss Peterson's class a few years ago, and we became friends. We were standing outside here, and I noticed it was gone. My diamond bracelet is gone."

"Calm down. Let's go back inside and look for it. It may have fallen off."

"No, it had a safety clasp. Someone took it."

The detective led the woman and her husband back into the auditorium. Several minutes later they returned empty-handed.

"Ma'am, we'll check the lost and found. If it's not there, come down to the station with me and we'll file a report."

Susan pulled her coat tighter around herself. *A murder? Stolen jewelry? What kind of town did Emily and Henry move into?*

Henry suggested heading back to the house. By the time they left, most of the crowd had already gone home. When they passed the cabin where Kiki and Buzz lived, Henry said, "What's he doing there? Look, Peewee's van is in their driveway."

"Plotting to get us to sell, no doubt," said Emily.

"That man has a peewee-sized brain if he hasn't yet gotten the message that we're here to stay. Let him waste his time all he wants."

Chapter 10

The next morning, Emily once again prepared a breakfast feast. Susan smelled bacon the moment her eyes opened. She and Mike went into the dining room.

"Grab a muffin. The eggs will be ready in a minute," said Emily.

Henry was reading the newspaper and sipping coffee. Chester the cat hung out at Emily's feet hoping for a bite of bacon.

"So, Emily, maybe the killer was after Martha after all? Noah heard her arguing with her boyfriend the night before the murder. He even slapped her."

"It is strange that she never mentioned a boyfriend. I heard Coralee say Martha's sister is staying at the inn. Maybe we can drop by this morning and have a chat."

"Emily, you stay clear. I've already come close to losing my wife once this week. I'm sure Detectives Wooster and O'Leary will be following that lead."

Susan remembered Gerald's strange behavior.

"Henry, you're a doctor. Let me ask you something about Gerald Reynolds. He got up right in the middle of the ceremony, remember? And he pulled out his wallet before he and Morgan even ordered their food at the inn the other night. Emily mentioned dementia."

"I'd say he's showing the signs, but without an actual exam and workup, I can't say."

"I've heard people with Alzheimer's can get violent," said Susan.

"They lose their inhibitions, might say things unfiltered, but actual violence? I don't think so. If you're thinking Gerald planned to kill Emily and you're thinking dementia, I will say I doubt he'd have had the capacity to plan it out. The police say the killer brought the weapon to the crime scene. The killer also planned to attack when he knew everyone would be at the inauguration. Someone with dementia would've had a hard time pulling it off."

"Joe told us Morgan and Gerald saved seats at the inauguration but then showed up late to the ceremony."

"Emily, he could have tried to wander off and Morgan had to get him back. That's pretty common with Alzheimer's patients. Who knows?"

Henry continued reading the paper while Mike helped himself to another muffin. Emily brought eggs to the table.

"Well, what do you know," said Henry. "Here's an article about Peter Taglieri of Peewee Miniatures. Says he's being investigated for misappropriating funds back in his last endeavor."

"I knew there was something criminal about him." Emily dished out the eggs.

"It's probably just the tip of the iceberg," said Susan. "Can I borrow your laptop, Emily?"

"Of course."

After they finished breakfast, Susan googled Peter Taglieri.

"Emily, look at all these articles." She scrolled through. "He was arrested for his involvement in a Ponzi scheme back in Arizona. Went on trial. He was convicted, but…"

"But what?" asked Mike.

"He was released on a technicality. Swarms of investors lost their shirts. This guy is ruthless. Look at this article. He moved on and started another miniature home community in Illinois. Says he was suspected of initiating yet another pyramid scheme out there. When suspicions arose, he sold the company and moved to Vermont. He moved here!"

"An unscrupulous businessman like him wouldn't let anything or anyone get in his way. If he couldn't convince us to sell, maybe he thought he'd kill me and then you'd move. Or maybe he planned to kill you too."

Susan nodded her head. "We did see his van heading toward Emily's office on the news report about the inauguration."

"Girls, that's a big leap. Besides, weren't we just discussing Martha's boyfriend as the killer? Weren't we saying he might have actually meant to kill her and not Emily?" said Mike.

"That's also a leap," said Henry. "And so is the idea that Gerald Reynolds did it. I doubt he'd be capable of planning a murder, like I said."

"But Morgan's earring was found under the office door."

"Susan, we haven't had that confirmed. The police were looking into it, remember?"

Right on cue, there was a knock at the door. Henry answered it. "Detective Wooster. We were just talking about you."

"I have a few questions for Susan Wiles if you don't mind."

"Of course not. Come in. Let me take your coat. Want some coffee?"

"No, thanks."

Susan said, "Nice to see you again, Detective."

"Mrs. Wiles, you said you found the earring stuck under Mrs. Fox's office door, correct?"

"Yes, that's right."

"And that was the first day we released the crime scene?"

"That's right. I'm surprised the police didn't find it earlier. Or the cleaning crew."

"It was wedged under the door. Must have gotten stuck the day of the murder; otherwise, it would have been found by the custodian. Did you happen to see Morgan Reynolds in the building the day you went over there?"

"Morgan Reynolds. It's her earring. I was right, wasn't I? Feathers and beads—just her style. Emily said she always wears…"

"Susan, just answer his question," said Mike.

"No, we didn't see her that day." Both she and Emily shook their heads.

After the detective left, Susan said, "I knew it was hers. Now don't you agree Morgan was in the building?"

Chapter 11

Susan and Emily drove to the inn, while Henry took Mike on another snowshoeing adventure. When the women arrived, the breakfast rush was over, and they found Coralee collapsed on the lobby sofa, feet perched on a floral hassock.

"Emily and Susan, can I get you some breakfast?"

"No, we already ate. Besides, you look exhausted. Busy morning?"

"No, Emily. The breakfast rush was rather light. It's just that I didn't sleep well. I waited up half the night for Noah. He never said he was going out. I didn't hear him climb the stairs until after two a.m."

"Did you ask him where he was?" said Emily.

"He said he was in his room all night long. Why did he lie to me? I hope it's not starting again."

"What's starting again?" said Emily.

"When Noah was a teenager, he was in and out of trouble with the law. Shoplifting, drunk driving, for a time he was even a suspect in the Ashley Young disappearance."

Susan's ears perked up. "Really? He knew Ashley?"

"Yes. As a teen, he worked at the university doing lawn maintenance in the summer, shoveling and plowing during the winter. Ashley was a student there, older than him, of course."

"Why was he a suspect?" asked Susan.

"They were friends. They hung out together when she was between classes. She even helped him pass high school Algebra, smart girl that she was. The day she disappeared, someone saw him talking to Ashley. They said it looked as though they were arguing out in the parking lot by her car."

"That doesn't prove anything, right, Susan?" said Emily.

"How reliable was the witness? Did they see Noah abduct her? Drive away with her?"

"No, of course not. The police dropped it after a while. They had no evidence tying him into her disappearance. Besides, they were leaning towards her running away voluntarily."

Noah came down the stairs wearing sweats. His hair was uncombed as if he'd just rolled out of bed.

"Hey, Mom. Any hot breakfast left?"

"No, you missed your chance. There's cereal in the kitchen. Don't you have class this morning?"

"Yeah. Guess I'm going to be late."

Susan asked, "Noah, did you go to the inauguration ceremony the other day? I heard it was quite an event."

"Yeah, I was there for most of it. The speeches got long, so I slipped out before the traffic started. Almost no cars on the road except for Dr. Sommers. I passed him as I was leaving the parking lot, though I couldn't figure out why he'd be showing up right at the end."

Noah headed to the kitchen. Susan heard the beep of the microwave and assumed he'd heated up something better than cereal.

Emily said, "Coralee, is Martha's sister still here?"

"Ellen Peterson? Yes, she's out on the porch, bundled up with a blanket and a book. I brought coffee out to her a little bit ago. Do you need her for something?"

"We just wanted to chat, tell her how much Martha meant to me."

Susan and Emily went outside and found Ellen Peterson in a rocking chair on the porch, book in hand, just as Coralee had said.

"Ellen Peterson? I'm Emily Fox. Martha was my coworker and good friend."

Ellen stood up and shook her hand. "Yes, Martha spoke of you often. You're the one who found her, right?"

"Unfortunately, yes. I can't get the image out of my mind. I'm missing her so much already. It won't be the same at school without her."

Ellen pulled out a handkerchief and blew her nose. She was older than Martha but had the same auburn hair and fair skin. Susan didn't have a sister although these days relatives had been popping up out of the woodwork, but she imagined how hard it must be to lose one.

Susan said, "I hope the police find her killer soon. It seems like everyone loved Martha. Do you have any idea who may have wanted to kill her?"

"She had a new boyfriend. She was rather elusive in giving me details, but I got the feeling things were going south. She mentioned finding out something disturbing about him. She was afraid to tell him she wanted to break things off."

"Did she tell him? Do you think he came after her?" said Susan.

"I don't know. I told all of this to Detective Wooster and his pretty partner. They were going to look into it. It's getting a bit too chilly out here. If you'll excuse me..."

"Of course," said Emily. "Again, my sincere condolences."

Emily and Susan headed back to the Jeep. "Susan, do you mind if we stop by my office? I have to teach my class tomorrow, and with all that's happened, I don't know which way is up. I want to get a few things together."

"Of course. You know, you said Ashley Young's parents still live in the area. Do you think it may be worth paying them a visit?"

"They are still here, but what would I hope to accomplish?"

"It's coming up on the tenth anniversary of their daughter's death, and you are writing a book suggesting it wasn't a simple case of a runaway. If the killer was in fact after you, rather than Martha, what reason would he have? Preventing the truth from coming out?"

"Well, there's the whole Peewee Miniatures drama. You found those articles proving Peter Taglieri broke the law and got off on a technicality. And Kiki and Buzz want us to sell. Sarah Kimberly, the adjunct instructor in Martha's basic course, was none too happy with her. And don't forget about Morgan Reynolds. You found her earring at the crime scene. Then there's her crazy husband."

"The crazy husband could be so hard to deal with that Morgan snapped and tried to kill you. But what about your book? Someone broke into your office and stole the audiotapes from the interviews. With the anniversary of Ashley's disappearance coming up, maybe someone who is still in the area abducted her and wants to remain in the shadows."

"Okay. Let's drive out to the Youngs' after we're done. I've spoken to them on the phone several times. Even had a taped interview, but, of course, that's gone. I'll let them know we're coming."

Emily called Ashley's parents from the car before going to her office. As soon as they opened the door to the building, a terrible noise flooded the hall.

"What's that? Oh, no! It's Gerald Reynolds. He's hacking my door with an ax! Call the police!"

Joe Sommers was in the hallway. He grabbed Gerald's arm and struggled to pull the ax away.

"Joe, what's going on?" Susan and Emily also grabbed Gerald's arm. Between the three of them, they wrestled the ax away. Joe pinned Gerald to the wall.

Morgan ran into the hallway. "What are you doing to my husband? Let him go."

"Do you see the ax on the floor? You're asking what we're doing to him? He was hacking up my office door. It took three of us to stop him," said Emily.

"Please, he can't help it. He's ill and doesn't know what he's doing."

"Ill, how?" asked Emily.

"He has a specific form of dementia. It's like Alzheimer's and Parkinson's rolled into one. He can't help himself."

"Then why is he out in public, Morgan? He belongs in a place where he can get help."

"He lost his job, remember? No insurance will cover him now, and I can't afford to put him in a facility. If they had just kept him on here a while longer, he could have made it to Medicare. As it is, he's too young."

"Emily said, "I'm so sorry, Morgan. I had no idea things were so bad."

Two police officers ran through the door. "What's going on? Are you all okay?"

"It's fine now, said Emily. But this man needs a doctor. Can you bring him to the hospital?"

"Do you want to press charges?"

"No one was hurt, and the college can replace the door. I'm not pressing charges."

The police escorted Morgan and Gerald out of the building. Emily unlocked what was left of her office door and everyone entered.

"Joe, did you know Gerald was sick?"

"No, but that explains the shaking and odd behavior. I saw the two of them coming in late to the inauguration ceremony. Maybe you were right, Emily. Maybe Gerald tried to run away and Morgan had to fetch him back."

"And it explains his behavior at the inn the other night too," said Susan.

"You know, I saw them both here in this building the morning before the ceremony."

"Joe, you didn't mention that before," said Emily.

"I forgot until now."

"If they were in the building then, that explains Morgan's earring. It must have dropped while they were in the hallway."

"Or in your office," said Joe.

Detective Wooster knocked on the broken door. "I heard what happened and came to check on you. Are you all okay?"

"Yes," said Emily. "Luckily, Joe Sommers is a regular gym goer. He got the ax away from Gerald. But I hope the college gets the door repaired quickly."

Susan stood up. "Detective, we think Morgan and Gerald were here the day Martha was murdered. It was her earring I found, right?"

The detective cleared his throat. "Yes, it was. You were right, Mrs. Wiles."

"And Gerald was holding an ax."

"An ax." The detective scratched his head.

"What's wrong, Detective?" Susan saw by his expression that something was puzzling him.

"It's just that we got back the coroner's report, and the murder weapon looks like a heavy piece of pipe. Lead particles were found on Mrs. Peterson's skull. It wasn't an ax. If Gerald was the killer and he owned an ax, why wouldn't he have used it? Where would he get a pipe?"

Emily said, "With his dementia, Gerald may have thought he was killing me. I know he was angry about losing his job. God knows he was strong enough to have done it. Look how hard it was to pry away the ax."

"Come to think of it, Gerald was holding something that day. It looked like a piece of silver pipe," said Joe.

"My husband is a doctor," said Emily, "and he doesn't think someone with Gerald's degree of dementia could have planned out a murder, even bringing his own murder weapon."

"People with dementia have times when they are perfectly lucid," argued Joe. "Maybe that was one of those times. Martha could have been in on it too."

"Martha's a hippie at heart," said Emily. "She's all about peace and nonviolence. And I just think Gerald is too sick to have done it."

"Ill or not," said Susan, "personally, I think we were just face to face with Martha's killer. Or killers."

Chapter 12

Ashley Young's parents lived in a secluded farmhouse about an hour away from Sugarbury Falls. A row of bare maple trees lined the long driveway leading to the front door. The house itself was small and needed a coat of paint. Smoke billowed from the chimney.

"Mrs. Fox, come in," said Mrs. Young.

Mrs. Young had her blond hair pulled back and wore no makeup. The profound stress she'd suffered over the past decade had etched her face with wrinkles and worry lines.

"This is my dear friend, Susan Wiles. She and her husband came up for a visit."

"I wanted to tag along and see a little more of this gorgeous area," added Susan.

Susan and Emily followed Mrs. Young into the living room. Mr. Young, a thin gentleman with a beard, was sitting in a recliner next to the fireplace.

"Can I get you some coffee?" asked Mrs. Young.

"No thanks. We're good," said Emily. She and Susan sat on the plaid sofa.

"We heard about the murder in Sugarbury Falls," said Mr. Young. "Is that why you came? Do you think it's related to Ashley's disappearance?"

"Mr. Young, it's possible. Also, all my audiotapes were stolen. Someone, namely Ashley's abductor, may still be out there and not happy that a book is being written taking the position foul play was involved."

Mrs. Young reached into the coffee table drawer. "I was going to call you. I want to show you something. Look, it's a postcard with a Mexico postmark."

Emily took the postcard and read it aloud:

"Dear Mom and Dad, I know it's been a while, but I wanted to touch base and reassure you that all is well. I've got a great job and wonderful husband, but can't come back to the states for reasons I don't want to get into. All my love, Ashley."

"You must be so relieved," said Susan.

"No, actually quite the opposite. That isn't Ashley's handwriting. Besides, if all were well, she would have called long ago. Ashley loved us and never would have let us worry all these years. And she wouldn't in a million years have gotten married without us there."

"And why now?" said Mr. Young. "Why didn't she let us know ten years ago?"

Susan said, "Someone's worried that the whole case will come to light again. They are trying to dissuade anyone from digging into her disappearance."

"Let's go over this once again. Did Ashley know anyone who may have wanted to harm her," asked Emily.

"Like I told you before, she didn't have a boyfriend, but on Valentine's Day prior to her disappearance, she received a flower delivery and a card. She tore the card into pieces and threw the flowers right into the trash. When her mother asked her who they were from, she said she didn't want to talk about it."

"Then there was that kid she was tutoring in algebra. She said he followed her everywhere around school, and it creeped her out. She was going to quit tutoring."

"Did she break it off?" said Emily.

"I don't know. That was shortly before she disappeared."

Mr. Young said, "Did my wife tell you about the package?"

"What package?"

"Not long after Ashley disappeared, we received a small package. Inside was a locket that belonged to Ashley."

"It belonged to my mother," added Mrs. Young. "When Ashley turned eighteen, her grandmother gave it to her. Ashley had been so upset when she thought she'd lost it."

"Are you sure it was the same locket?" asked Emily.

"Positive. There had been a picture of Ashley's grandfather inside, but it's missing now."

"Don't forget to tell her about the note," said Mr. Young.

"Yes, there was a note. Typed. It said, *Keep it safe.*"

Emily said, "*Keep it safe*? Did you show this note to the police?"

"We did. Her father insisted we do that right away. They dismissed it. If anything, they thought it was proof Ashley had left of her own free will and was returning it to us to pass down to future generations. But that made no sense at all to us. Ashley was our only child."

Emily and Susan got up to leave. Mrs. Young took Emily's hand.

"Please help us find out what happened to our daughter. I know you always believed our side."

"I won't stop until I get answers," said Emily. "I want to know what happened as much as you do."

Chapter 13

"That was a productive visit," said Susan.

"Yes, it was. I wish she would have called me when she got the postcard or the package."

Emily and Susan turned into Maplewood. As they pulled closer to the house, Emily said, "Look, there's Henry and Mike."

Henry and Mike, wearing snowshoes, were standing outside of the barn with Kurt Olav. Emily parked the Jeep beside the barn.

Susan said, "How's the snowshoeing going?"

"Gets easier with practice," said Mike. "Bending down on snowshoes, however, is a different story."

Henry brushed snow from the doorjamb with his glove. "Someone's been in here. There are marks like the door was pried open. We were about to go inside."

Kurt said, "I told you I saw the door open. Last night, I saw someone walking away from the barn. It was late. I couldn't sleep, so I came out for a walk. Me and Prancer."

The foursome entered the dark barn. The door creaked, and a sliver of sunlight shone on the floor. Cobwebs hung from the corners of the walls, and old farm equipment, which had once been used to keep horses, filled the stalls. Susan sneezed.

"Let's each start at a corner and work our way into the middle," said Henry. He grabbed the flashlight.

Emily asked, "What is it we're looking for?"

"Any sign that someone's been in here. Kurt, you check the stalls."

Susan wished she'd worn her gloves. Every time she touched the barn wall, her hands got caked with dirt. She ran her hand along the boards. "Ouch!" She clutched her hand. Blood trickled from her palm.

Mike ran over. "Are you okay? What happened?"

"Scraped my hand on a rusty nail. Good thing I'm up-to-date on my tetanus shot."

Emily fetched hand sanitizer and a Band-Aid from her purse. Susan cleaned the wound as best she could and went back to work.

"Hey, I found something," said Kurt. "Here in the stall." He knelt down under a wheelbarrow.

Henry said, "What's that?" He shone the flashlight on a metal tackle box that was half-buried in the dirt.

"Open it," said Susan.

Kurt pulled on the lid. "It's locked with a padlock. Hand me something to pry it off with."

Henry searched for a tool. "Here, try this screwdriver."

Kurt stuck the screwdriver under the lid. "I can't get it off."

Mike grabbed a rusty hammer and wacked at the padlock. Finally he was able to open the box.

All eyes stared as Mike lifted the lid and opened the box.

"It's jewelry," said Emily. She fingered a diamond bracelet.

Susan took out an emerald ring and a strand of pearls. "We have to call the police."

"Not so fast," said Kurt. "They'll pick up the jewelry and try to return the pieces to their owners, but I know this town. The police don't have the manpower to track down the thief. Especially not in the middle of a murder investigation. Let's do this the Minnesota way."

"What's that?" said Susan.

"You'll see. Meet me here after dark."

* * * * *

After dark, Susan, Emily, Henry, and Mike met Kurt in front of the barn. Without a visible moon or stars, the night sky was eerie and foreboding. The group huddled together in the cold.

Susan could see her own breath as she exhaled, asking the question she knew they all had. "How do you know he's going to show up?"

Kurt said, "Virtually every night I've seen someone out here."

Henry said, "Why didn't you say anything before?"

"I didn't see him stealing or vandalizing, so I kept my mouth shut. Now we know the guy's a thief."

"Or the woman," said Emily. "Let's take our post."

All four hid inside the barn. Susan kept her phone out, gambling on the service working if she needed to call the police. Besides, the glow from the phone was reassuring in the otherwise pitch-black barn. She pulled a bag of chips from her coat pocket and offered them to the others.

"I see you came prepared for a stakeout," said Emily.

"It could be hours. Gotta keep up our energy."

Something scampered over Susan's feet. "Ahhh!"

"Shh!" said Henry.

"It… it… A rat just ran over my foot."

Henry turned on the flashlight. "It's just a mouse. See. He's scampering right into that hole."

"That's supposed to be reassuring?" said Susan. "Maybe he has an entire mouse family living here. And just because one critter was a mouse doesn't mean there aren't rats here too."

"My knees hurt," said Emily. "How long are we going to wait?"

"Shh!" said Henry. "I hear someone outside. Listen." He turned off the flashlight. The door creaked as it opened.

Susan's heart pounded, partially from fear and partially from excitement. It was too dark to see, so she relied on her sense of hearing. Footsteps came closer. Everyone held their breaths. The stall door creaked open. The girls were perched on either side of the stall. Susan felt someone brush right past them. She squeezed Emily's hand. All of a sudden, two flashlights shone on the perpetrator. Kurt grabbed him from behind and pinned his hands behind his back. Like a reflex, Susan called 911.

Emily said, "Noah! You're the thief!"

Susan said, "Coralee told us jewelry was stolen from the inn. And remember the lady at the service who said her diamond bracelet was missing?"

"I saw Coralee and Noah at the service. Poor Coralee!" said Emily.

"What were you thinking?" said Henry. "Stealing from your mom's guests?"

Noah struggled to get away, but Kurt held tight. Detectives Wooster and O'Leary, carrying flashlights, burst through the barn door.

"What have we got here?" said Detective Wooster.

"You can't prove anything," said Noah, struggling. "I was taking a walk, and I saw the door open. I was checking it out for the Foxes, that's all."

Susan dug through the box one more time before handing it to the police. What's this stuck in the corner? It's an old picture of an elderly man. It's cut in a heart shape, like to fit into a locket. "Emily, didn't Ashley Young's parents tell us Ashley lost a locket? One her grandmother handed down to her?"

"Yes, and someone sent the locket back to them."

"I'm sure, Detectives, you will find this photo fits the locket." Susan handed the photo to Detective Wooster, who sealed it in an evidence bag.

Detective O'Leary picked up the box. Detective Wooster cuffed Noah and walked toward the door.

"How did you all happen to be out here just when Noah came by?"

"Coincidence, I guess. I'm glad we were here. Not only do you have the jewel thief, I have a sneaking suspicion this young man was involved in Ashley Young's disappearance too," said Susan.

"We'll check it out. Go home, everyone. It's freezing out here."

Chapter 14

The next morning, Susan slept much later than usual. She and her friends were exhausted after the events of the previous night. After Noah had been arrested, they had gone down to the station to make statements, getting back home well after midnight.

"Good morning," said Emily. "Did you sleep as soundly as I did?" Chester was curled up on her lap.

"Yes, and I still need coffee to get me going. Where are the guys?"

"They went for a walk. Henry wanted to assess the damage to the barn door. He was hoping that between him and Mike they could avoid hiring an outsider to do the job."

Susan's phone vibrated. "It's Lynette."

Lynette was Susan's older child, a detective back in Westbrook, NY. She was married to Jason, a college professor, and they were parents to two-year-old Annalise.

"Lynette, how's Annalise? I miss her so much."

"She's great. You need to start doing FaceTime with her. You know, Jonathan started that. Ever since he found out he has a grandchild, he calls almost every day. Annalise calls him *Papa* and kisses the screen good-bye when they hang up. He sent her a pack of coloring books in the mail yesterday with a box of those extra big crayons."

"I couldn't be more thrilled. What's going on with the adoption?"

"They interviewed our friends last week, and we passed with flying colors. Tomorrow, we have another home study."

"Before you know it, you'll be traveling to China to bring home Annalise's new sister! Make sure you get up and walk around on the plane. I saw on Dr. Oz that you can get blood clots in your legs if you sit for a long time."

"Okay, Mom. Let me write this down. Walk around the plane so I don't get blood clots."

"Be sarcastic if you want, but look it up and you'll see it's a real thing."

Susan filled Lynette in on recent events in Sugarbury Falls. Lynette teased her that she had some sort of internal magnet that attracted murders and warned her yet again to be careful. While Susan had been talking, Emily had also been on the phone.

"Everything good with Lynette?"

"Great. They're developing a real relationship with my biological father Jonathan. He's already made more effort in his short time as a grandfather than Audrey has as a grandmother."

"But Audrey has been preoccupied, right?"

"Lovesick is more like it. Disgusting at her age with that creep Richard, Jonathan's own brother."

"Let me see if I have this straight. Your mother is marrying your uncle?"

"Yep."

"Mothers. I'm glad Henry and I never had children to mess up. Well, that was Coralee on the phone. She's really upset, understandably. She asked if we could stop by the inn since she can't leave. Noah was capable of running the business in her absence, but now…"

"Say no more. Let's go."

Susan grabbed her coat while Emily put together a tin of baked goods. It was one of those cold, clear days.

The sky was deep blue, and the sun reflected off the snow. Coralee was waiting in the lobby.

Emily hugged her. "I'm so sorry. I can't imagine finding out your son was the jewel thief."

"I knew he wasn't perfect. He'd had his troubles as a teen, but this? I don't know what to say. I should have seen signs. Maybe if his father were still alive things would be different."

"Don't blame yourself. You've done an incredible job balancing the business with motherhood. He always had a roof over his head and food in his belly. It's nothing you did."

"Thanks, Emily. Wish I could believe that."

They followed Coralee into the dining room, which was pretty much empty now that the breakfast rush was over.

"I have to tell you something," said Coralee. "Martha Peterson, the teacher who was killed, came to see me. She told me Noah was in trouble. She caught him in her office one day. He was walking out with her watch. She often took off her watch when she had a lot of typing to do. Said it got in her way."

"What did you do?"

"I'm ashamed to say I didn't believe her. I said, like most mothers, that my son wouldn't do such a thing. She was very calm, in spite of my angry tone. She said she'd talk to Noah herself. It was just a few days before Martha was killed."

Emily said, "Are you worried that Noah killed Martha because she was going to report him to the police?"

"I... I don't know," Coralee replied. "A jewel thief, I can picture that. But a murderer? I can't believe he'd do that, but I'm not sure I know my own son anymore."

Emily and Susan turned their heads when Joe Sommers walked in with a young woman. Emily whispered, "She's a student."

Susan mouthed, "Oh, my."

Holding menus, Coralee motioned to Joe and the young woman to follow her. "Come in. Table for two?"

"That would be lovely. This is one of our English Department adjuncts Bridgette McLain. She teaches basic comp. I'm helping her with her dissertation. We're having an informal brainstorming session."

"Joe, don't you have a class now?" said Emily.

"I'm letting one of the new adjuncts handle it."

"Who would that be?"

"Sarah Kimberly. Now that poor Martha is gone, Sarah needs a new mentor, and since I've taken over the basic comp class from Martha, there's more work to be done."

And I bet you've got some of your own, thought Susan. *I don't know if it's appropriate to be doling out your work to an adjunct. Work to be done, indeed.*

"What can I get for you," said Coralee. "The special this morning is eggs with salsa."

"Huevos Rancheros. Love it. Had them every morning while I was on my vacation in Cancun last month." Joe shut his menu. "Bring some for the young lady also. Emily, why don't you and Susan have a seat while you wait for Coralee."

I wonder if he took this girl on vacation with him? Or another young adjunct, perhaps?

Emily and Susan grabbed their coffee and sat down.

"So, how's the book coming along, Emily?" asked Joe.

"I had a bit of a setback, but I'll get back on track. Going to reinterview some witnesses," Emily said.

"You know, I don't know if I ever told you this, but that young boy who worked on campus, Coralee's son,

I'm sure I saw him talking to Ashley Young the day she disappeared. They were in the parking lot, arguing. I heard them out my window. Then I saw him grab Ashley's arm. She ran away from him, but he ran after her."

"Then what?"

"I had to leave to teach a class. That's all I saw."

"You never told me that," said Emily. "Or the police, did you?"

"Guess I pushed it back in my mind. On the news this morning, I heard the boy was arrested. Jogged my memory," Joe replied.

Coralee came in with two steaming platters of spicy eggs. "Were you saying something about Noah?"

Susan shook her head behind Coralee as if to say to Joe, she has enough to worry about without hearing that now.

Joe took a bite of his eggs. "Yum, just like I remember them. Didn't realize you had a knack for authentic Mexican cooking. I was just saying I heard about your son on the news. I'm so sorry, Coralee. I know a good lawyer if you need a name."

"Thanks, Joe. I'll be in the lobby if you need me. Without Noah, I have to run the whole show here. I think I heard the door." She rushed off.

I feel so terrible for Coralee. It's bad enough that her son has been arrested, but she has to run the whole inn by herself now," said Joe. "And lawyer fees can take a big chunk of money. She has to be worried sick."

Emily and Susan followed Coralee into the lobby and waited while she checked in a guest.

Susan whispered to Emily, "Is Joe Sommers a bit of a sleaze or what? Taking an adjunct half his age to breakfast? I sure hope she didn't spend the night with him."

"Susan! Joe isn't like that at all. He's more like a father figure to his students. He's super friendly, and sometimes maybe it comes off wrong."

"If you say so. Maybe I have it all wrong."

Coralee showed the new guests to their room. When she came back downstairs, she said, "Sorry about that."

"Coralee, you look like there's something else you want to say," said Emily.

Coralee looked at the floor. "I'm worried that Martha's murder may not be the only one Noah is involved in. That girl, Ashley Young. The night she disappeared, Noah never came home. He didn't come back to the inn until the next morning."

Susan said, "Don't go jumping to conclusions. We know Noah stole jewelry. That's all we know for sure. Thinking he killed Martha Peterson and maybe Ashley Young... That's a big leap. Don't let your imagination run wild just because you're doubting Noah right now."

Then again, Susan thought, *I saw Noah's wet backpack the night Martha was killed. And possibly blood on his hands.*

"I guess you're right. What kind of a mother am I?"

Sirens blared from outside. The three women ran out onto the porch where they watched two different police cars whiz by. Joe and Bridgette followed them.

"What's happening?" said Joe. "Look, a third police car."

"I wonder what's going on?" said Susan. Please, God. Not another murder. I'm beginning to believe Lynette is right about me. She rubbed her hand over her middle. I am a murder magnet."

Chapter 15

"Coralee, let's go inside and turn on the TV. Maybe there's some information."

"Good idea, Emily." Coralee led them into the den. As soon as she turned on the set, there it was. Breaking news.

"Oh my God," said Coralee. "That's Ashley Young's car! After ten years, they found her car."

The newscaster cut to a shot of an old barn behind a dilapidated cabin. The Peewee Miniatures van was in the driveway along with several police cars.

"That's Mrs. Anderson's farm. Poor dear is in a wheelchair. Has been for years. I hope she's okay," said Coralee.

The newscaster announced that the owner was recently deceased and the property had been purchased by Peewee Miniatures. When the new owner checked the barn, he found the car, which was traced back to Ashley Young.

"Deceased? I didn't even know. I'll bet the car's been there the whole time."

"Really, Coralee? But how could she not know there was a car in her barn all this time? You mean she hadn't been in her barn for ten years?" said Emily.

"She's been in that wheelchair as long as I can remember. She had a part-time nurse; that's the only person I ever saw over there. I can believe no one had been in that barn all that time."

Coralee turned off the TV. "More bad news. I guess Peewee has another chunk of land to build on now."

"Well," said Emily, "they're not getting ours and I know you aren't selling, Coralee."

"Over my dead body. Even if running this place without Noah kills me."

Emily and Susan got back in the Jeep. They could see flashing lights from down the road as they drove away from the inn.

"Peter Taglieri must be gloating about now," said Emily. "Mrs. Anderson was never going to sell her place, no matter how much she was pressured. When she died, I suspect her son inherited the place. He lives down in Florida. I'm sure he was more than anxious to unload the property."

"There's definitely something shady about Peter Taglieri," said Susan. "When we get back to your place, I'd like to do a little more research."

Emily pulled into their driveway. Waiting at the door were Kiki and Buzz.

"Now are you going to sell?" said Buzz. "Looks like bad things happen to those who hold out. Just saw that poor Anderson woman on the news. In the end, Peewee wound up with the land."

"Is that a threat?" said Emily.

"More like some neighborly advice," said Buzz.

Emily and Susan went inside where they found Henry and Mike on the sofa.

"Did you see the news?" said Henry. "Mrs. Anderson is dead, and they found Ashley Young's car."

"Heard the sirens ourselves," said Emily. "Poor Coralee. Noah was arrested last night for stealing, and now she's worried he may have been involved in two murders."

"What? How is Noah connected to two murders?"

"He tried to steal Martha Peterson's watch. She caught him and threatened to go to the police, not long before she was found dead," said Emily.

"And both Ashley Young's parents and Joe Sommers confirmed a relationship between Noah and Ashley. Ashley's parents said she tutored him, but things were getting weird and Ashley stopped doing it. Joe said he saw the two of them arguing the day Ashley went missing."

Susan said, "You have even more proof for your book, Emily. Now that they found Ashley's car, that virtually rules out the theory she left voluntarily. Now if they could only find her body."

Mike gave her a look. She had to remember to be more sensitive.

"Her parents will be devastated if and when they find a body," said Henry.

Emily's phone vibrated. "It's Ashley Young's father." She took the phone and walked outside. When she came back, she said, "The police called the Youngs and told them about the car. They also told them about the locket. Mrs. Young remembered something and wants to talk to me."

"I'll take a ride up there with you," said Susan.

"Grab your coat, and let's go," said Emily.

Chapter 16

Emily turned on the windshield wipers to clear the snow flurries. The trip to the Youngs' cabin seemed closer now that she'd been out there a few times. She and Susan knocked on the door and were ushered inside. Takeout containers from the general store covered the coffee table. Newspapers littered the floor.

This latest piece of news has to have thrown them into a tizzy. My house would be a mess too under the circumstances, Susan thought.

"Thanks for coming so quickly," said Mrs. Young. "Can I get you some coffee?"

"We'd love some," said Emily.

Mrs. Young set up the coffee and returned to the living room. "The police brought us the photo that was in Ashley's locket to identify and told us they caught the thief. I'm sure it was the boy Ashley was tutoring."

"Yes," said Emily. "It was. On the phone, you said you remembered something important."

"Shortly before she went missing," said Mr. Young, "Ashley made a comment. Something about putting a crook behind bars. I told the police back then, but I didn't connect it with anything. Now I think she must have been talking about Noah Saunders. If Ashley was going to the police about him, Noah Saunders had a motive to kill her."

"The police will take that into consideration," said Emily. "For what it's worth, I don't think Noah is a killer."

"Well, there's one more thing that may or may not be important," continued the father. "Ashley was upset about a grade. She was always an A student but said one of her professors was giving her a hard time. She made a comment that he was taking advantage of his position. Like I said, I don't know if it's significant. I didn't even remember it until recently. I was going through her school memory box and saw report cards from elementary school. It made me think about her college grades, and then I remembered."

"Make sure you tell the police," said Emily. "Meanwhile, I can look at Ashley's transcript and see what classes she was taking."

Mrs. Young gave Emily a hug, "Thanks for supporting and believing us even back when you were still living in New York. You've invested a lot of years in our story."

"I want to see justice done," said Emily. "I knew from the start your daughter didn't leave on her own accord. This book will be finished, and the world will know the true story."

Emily and Susan set out for home. It was snowing a bit harder, and Emily drove slowly.

"Emily, look. That's Peter Taglieri's van. Peewee Miniatures. What's he doing way out here?"

"I don't know. This is far from the area he wants to build on. Do you mind if we stop by the college? I want to look up Ashley's courses the semester she went missing."

"I was thinking the same thing."

After a slow ride back to town, Emily pulled in front of the admissions and records building at St. Edwards. Now that second semester was underway, the office was eerily quiet. They walked up to the transcripts window and stated their request.

The woman behind the counter said, "I'm sorry, but we will need permission from her family. I can fax a form if you have a number."

"I know they have a fax machine. Over the years they've sent me documents and pictures to use in my book. I'll give them a call and get the number."

Emily called Mrs. Young. She heard the doorbell in the background over her phone.

"Excuse me a minute, someone's at the door." Mrs. Young was gone a few minutes, then came back to the phone and told Emily that Peter Taglieri was at the door. She gave Emily the fax number and ended the call.

"Peter Taglieri is at their house. What does he want from them?" asked Emily.

Susan said, "Taglieri? We passed his van, remember? He probably wants them to make you stop writing the book, especially since the car's been found. Again, who wants to move to a town where there's been multiple murders?"

"I'm sure he was up to no good. Let's do a little more digging when we get back home," suggested Susan.

Emily filled out the transcript request form and was disappointed to hear it would take up to a week to get the information she wanted.

When they got back to the Foxes,' Emily pulled out her laptop. She and Susan searched through every bit of information they could find on Peewee Miniatures and Peter Taglieri. Susan could see Emily was getting frustrated. She was getting rather frustrated herself trying to pull up the info on her phone. Even with her bifocals, it was challenge.

"You know, maybe we're going about this too linearly," said Susan. "Let's look at each purchase

Taglieri made prior to building his developments. Maybe it will lead us somewhere."

Emily searched and found a list of names. "Now what?"

"Let me have the computer." Susan typed, barely noticing the men had returned.

"What have you two been up to?" said Henry. He leaned two fishing poles and an ice saw against the wall. "Guess what Kurt told us?"

"What?" said Emily.

"I don't know how Kurt seems to pick up on things the way he does, but he heard Mrs. Anderson had been receiving threats just like we have. Threats about what would happen if she didn't sell her place. She had a note placed in her mailbox telling her time was running out and also had a rock thrown through her window. A note saying 'Sell or take the consequences' was taped to it."

"You've got to be kidding. We took a ride out to the Youngs' farm," said Emily. "On the way home, we passed Taglieri's van. Found out he paid the Youngs a visit. We were just doing a little more research." She nodded toward Susan.

"Aha!" said Susan. "Look what I found." She turned the screen to Emily. Mike and Henry leaned over her shoulder.

"Taglieri bought a property from a man named Tim Thompson. It was the last one he needed to build his previous development. Now look at this."

"Let us see," said Emily.

"Tim Thompson died under mysterious circumstances. Right after he died, Taglieri was able to purchase his land from a relative who had inherited it. Does that sound familiar?" Susan asked.

"If Henry and I died, that would be Taglieri's move," said Emily. "His van was spotted going in the opposite direction of the inauguration, remember? And do we know Mrs. Anderson died of natural causes? Knowing what Kurt told you, I'd say foul play was involved. Taglieri wound up with her place."

"Do you think he killed Ashley?" said Mike.

Emily answered, "He wasn't around back then. I'll bet he was as stunned as anyone to find her car in the barn. And I'm sure he was worried it would get out and bring negative publicity."

Susan stood up. "Let's examine our timeline. Martha is killed, but assume Taglieri was after Emily to either get the house or stop the book from being written. He killed Martha by mistake."

"Then he stole the interview tapes from my office," added Emily.

"He managed to knock off poor Mrs. Anderson and discovered the car in the barn," Susan continued. "Then he tried to get Ashley's parents to prevent you from writing the book."

Mike said, "There's no evidence connecting Taglieri to Martha's murder or to the break-in. You have to be careful to back up what you're saying."

"But, hun," argued Susan, "Taglieri's van was going *away* from the inauguration and *towards* Emily's office the afternoon Martha was killed."

"It's speculative at best," replied Mike.

"Looks like there are two suspects in the forefront," said Henry. "Noah Saunders and Peter Taglieri."

"Three," said Emily. "Martha's boyfriend is still under investigation."

Emily's phone vibrated and she answered it. "What, are you serious? You said no, right? Let me know if he contacts you again." Her face flushed with anger.

"What's wrong?" said Susan. "Who was that?"

"It was Mrs. Young," Emily said. "Remember how we heard Peter Taglieri at her door when we were on the phone last time?"

"Yes, when we were at the transcripts office," said Susan.

"He offered them a million dollars to take back permission for me to write the book. Says the publicity will hurt his business," Emily announced.

"See, Mike?" exclaimed Susan. "What a schmuck!" She turned to Emily. "The Youngs still want you to go ahead with the book, right?"

"More than ever," said Emily.

Chapter 17

Still dumbfounded at the gall of Peter Taglieri, Susan and Emily headed to the police station to update the detectives.

"After we're done, I need to stop by my office," said Emily. "It won't take long."

The station was smaller and older than the one in Westbrook where Lynette worked. Susan smelled coffee. Detective O'Leary was making copies. Detective Wooster was at his desk. "Can I help you, ladies?"

Emily said, "Detective, we found some information about Peter Taglieri. Before setting up shop here in Vermont, he profited from a mysterious death. Tim Thompson, the victim, owned land that Peter wanted. The man wouldn't sell. After his death, a relative inherited the place and sold it to Peewee Miniatures."

"Then Mrs. Anderson died. Emily told me Peewee wanted to buy her land, but she wouldn't sell either. We heard she'd received threats. Now she's dead. Her son didn't hesitate to unload the property."

"Even though we recently moved here, Henry and I have been spending summers up here with his family for many years. I remember Henry's mother talking about Mrs. Anderson's stubbornness. She admired her for it."

Susan said, "Now Taglieri can't convince Emily and Henry to sell. If he killed Emily, I'm sure he figured Henry wouldn't stay up here by himself."

"Or maybe he was planning on killing Henry too," said Emily.

"Mrs. Anderson died of natural causes," said Detective Wooster. "And we can't place Peter Taglieri at your office at the time of the murder. Calm down and trust us to do our job."

"Natural causes. I assume an autopsy was performed?" asked Susan.

Emily put her hand on Susan's shoulder and discreetly shook her head, but Susan ignored her. "Peter's van was heading away from the inauguration ceremony. That was the same day Martha was murdered. It was on the news. You have proof."

"It may be proof that the van was on the college grounds. We have nothing even hinting that Taglieri was at the office. Now, I have work to do. If you'll excuse me."

"Of course, Detective," said Emily.

She led Susan out to the car. "Susan, be careful. We don't want to get the police on our bad side. Off to St. Edwards. I have a stack of papers to grade. I'll grab them, and how about going over to the antique store afterward?"

"Sounds like fun," said Susan. She couldn't stop mulling over the information about Peter Taglieri. The man has a criminal record and needed to obtain Mrs. Anderson's land. Just like with Tim Thompson, the owner conveniently dies and—poof—Taglieri gets the land. *He still needs Emily and Henry's place*, reasoned Susan, *and then there's an attempt to kill Emily. Add to the mix the fact that Emily is writing a book, which would bring bad publicity to the town, discouraging potential buyers from purchasing tiny homes*. It was a quick ride, and soon they were on the college grounds. "Hey, isn't that your colleague?"

"Yes, that's Joe. Looks like he's heading to his office."

"The girl with him. We saw her at the inn, right? One of your department's adjuncts, Bridgette."

"Yes, that's her."

"They seem awfully friendly, walking so close like that. Look, he just gave her a swat on the butt!"

"Are you sure, Susan? Wait, you're right. He did it again. He has to be joking with her."

Susan and Emily pulled behind the office and went inside. Emily gathered her papers and checked her school e-mail. She drummed her fingers on the desk.

"What's wrong?"

"Darn, I have to fill this form out, but I'm not sure what code to put. Let's see if Joe made it to his office yet."

They walked down the hall, passing Bridgette on the way.

"Joe, I need some help." She fanned herself with the form.

"Anything. What do you need?"

"This is due tomorrow, and I have no idea what to put for the code."

"Here, I'll write it in."

Susan said, "It's really stuffy in here. Do you mind if I open the window?"

"I wouldn't mind, but that window doesn't open. It's been stuck shut for years. Where are you ladies heading?"

"Hitting the antique store," said Emily. "I'll see you tomorrow."

On the way back to her office, they passed the adjunct Sarah Kimberly who Emily had reported had been arguing with Martha before her murder. Emily said, "Hi, Sarah. How's your dissertation coming along?"

"Just great. Joe, I mean Dr. Sommers, says I'm on my way. Proposal is done, and I'm starting on my lit search. As a matter of fact, I'm heading over to the library now."

"Good to hear," said Emily. "At this rate, you'll be Dr. Kimberly in no time."

When they reached the car, Susan said, "Do we know for sure Morgan and Gerald aren't the killers?" She was leaning toward Taglieri, but in the back of her mind, she still suspected Gerald and wanted to go back over the possibilities.

"I don't think Gerald could have pulled it off," said Emily.

"Joe said he and Morgan came late to the inauguration ceremony," argued Susan.

"I have an idea," said Emily. "If it will make you feel better, we can stop by the publicity office. I'm sure they recorded the ceremony from start to finish, and we can see for ourselves."

Emily pulled in front of the main library where the publicity office was located. They walked past students working on computers and small groups who appeared to be working on projects. Emily knocked on the door. A film student on work-study manned the desk.

"Hi, Dr. Fox. What can I help you with?"

"We want to see the footage from the inauguration. Do you have it here?"

"Sure." He typed in the info. "Here's the link. You can use that computer by the window."

Emily and Susan sat down and connected to the footage.

"I recognize most of these people," said Emily. They watched for several minutes. "There's Morgan and Gerald."

"The ceremony hasn't started yet, and they're going in now. Look, they have seats. There's Sarah Kimberly.

She made it before the ceremony started. And look. There's the Peewee van like we saw on the news."

They watched the entire inauguration.

"We never see the van return and no sign of Peter Taglieri inside."

"Morgan and Gerald are leaving with everyone else. So is Sarah Kimberly. That gives them an alibi for the murder. We can cross them off the list."

"Mission accomplished. Let's go antiquing."

Chapter 18

The scenic drive to the antique store took them around the lake to a small downtown area. Cobblestone Main Street was comprised of a used bookstore, a general store, a post office, and a café. Antique-style streetlights hung at regular intervals. A copper sculpture of a maple tree surrounded by shrubs and flanked by two park benches formed a square in the middle of the area.

"During the summer, there's a farmers' market here every weekend," said Emily. "And you see people eating bag lunches on the benches."

"It's an adorable little town."

"Don't use the word *adorable*. Peter Taglieri uses it in his pitch for his future tiny house community."

"How presumptuous is he?"

"Very. And knowing how he always seems to get his way, I fear for the future of Sugarbury Falls. Even if Henry and I don't sell, watch him try building somewhere nearby where he can bully the landowners into relinquishing their property. Here's the antique store."

Paradoxically clean yet dusty, the antique store smelled of damp, old books. The shiny, tiled entranceway and front window sparkled, and a hint of a residual bleach aroma greeted them. When the bell over the door signaled their entrance, the owner emerged from the back.

"Hi, Emily. Who's your friend?"

"Susan Wiles. An old friend from back in New York. She's a retired teacher, here with her husband, Mike."

"I hope you're enjoying your visit. Can I help you find anything in particular?"

"Just browsing for now."

Susan and Emily worked their way around the store. In the furniture area, Susan found a treasure. "Emily, look at this cradle. It's so sweet. It would be perfect for my new grandbaby."

"It's beautiful. You can get Mike to paint her name on it."

"Oh, and look, a rocking chair. Look at the intricate carvings on the back. Flowers and hearts, so sweet."

"Doesn't Lynette have one from Annalise?"

"This is for my house. For when my granddaughters come visit."

The shop owner rang up the purchases. "I love this cradle. If I had grandchildren of my own, it never would have made it out to the floor. Good thing you've got a Jeep."

Susan suddenly remembered they'd driven to Vermont in a Prius. "Oh no. Maybe I'll just take the cradle."

"No way," said Emily. "We'll keep it at our house, and we'll bring it to you next time we visit. I'm sure it will be before the baby comes."

The shop owner helped them load the purchases into the Jeep. As they were about to leave, Susan recognized someone leaving the bookstore across the street.

"Emily, isn't that Martha Peterson's sister?"

"Sure is. I'm surprised she's still here." When she moved closer, they greeted her.

"Are you getting all the arrangements wrapped up?" asked Emily. "I know it must be hard. I can go through her office for you if you'd like."

"That would be helpful. I'd like to get back home within the next few days. Do you know if the police ever found Martha's boyfriend?"

"Not that we've heard," said Emily. "Of course it's not like they share all their info with us. I have a class in the morning. I'll go over to her office after that."

By the time they got back to Emily's, it was nearly time for dinner. Emily parked the Jeep, then got the men to help unload the new treasures. They were surprised to find Kurt in the living room sharing a beer with the guys.

"We have some treasures in the car. Can you help us carry them?"

Kurt, Henry, and Mike followed the girls outside. Mike and Henry carried the cradle into the house. When they returned, all three men struggled to get the rocking chair out of the Jeep.

Henry said, "Where are we going to put this? I don't think there's a free corner left in our place. It's too heavy to bring up to the loft."

"What about the barn?" asked Emily. "Susan and Mike are taking the cradle home with them, but we'll have to store the rocker until our next trip to see them."

"The barn it is then," said Henry. "Come on, Kurt. You grab that end."

Susan and Emily held open the barn door while the men carried in the rocker. Susan looked down at the floor. She saw a partial shoe print near one of the stalls.

"Look down there. The last time we were in here, the night we caught Noah, there were definitely no footprints on the floor. I looked."

Henry said, "No one has been in here since that night. It must be Noah's."

"Noah wears those heavy work boots," said Emily. "He was wearing them the night we caught him. This looks more like a sneaker print. I'm going to call Detective Wooster."

"In the meantime, let's go inside," said Henry. "Come with us, Kurt. I'll make coffee."

"You know," said Kurt, "I thought I was going crazy, but last night when I was out walking with Prancer, I could have sworn I saw a shadow by the barn. Figured I was imagining things."

Emily said, "Noah is sitting in a jail cell. Do you think he had an accomplice?"

Later after the coffee was made, Detectives Wooster and O'Leary knocked on the door.

"Come on in," said Henry. "We called because our friend Susan noticed a print on the barn floor. She swears it wasn't there the night Noah was arrested."

"I'm glad she noticed it. We took pictures of the crime scene, and I checked them before coming over. Mrs. Wiles is right. The print wasn't there the night we arrested Noah. It has to be more recent."

Emily said, "Do you think Noah had an accomplice? Have you had any more reports of stolen jewelry?"

"Not since we arrested Noah Saunders. We'll take an impression of the print and see if there's any other new evidence out there."

"I thought I saw someone out there last night," said Kurt. "It was just a shadow, and I figured it was nothing, but in light of the shoe print…"

"Thanks. Keep on the alert. If someone else is going in that barn, we'll catch him," said Detective O'Leary.

Chapter 19

Susan thought about the footprint while tossing and turning most of the night. *Besides Noah, who else would possibly have reason to be in Emily and Henry's barn? Was Peter Taglieri checking to be sure there wasn't a surprise in there before knocking off Emily and Henry?*

The next morning, Susan drank an extra cup of coffee in hopes of compensating for her sleepless night. The sugary syrup on top of Emily's homemade pancakes boosted her blood sugar, and after breakfast, she felt ready to take on the day.

Henry and Mike went out for another round of ice fishing. Emily took Susan with her to the college while she taught her class. Afterward, they kept their promise to Martha Peterson's sister and went to Martha's office.

"I'll start with her files," said Emily. "Why don't you get the books?"

It's eerie going through things that were recently used by someone who is now dead. Susan went through the bookshelf and packed the personal books into a box. "Hey, was this always here?" She picked up a heavy trophy and turned it over.

"Looking for blood?" said Emily.

"Well, actually... I don't see any." Susan packed the trophy with the books. While she was working, she heard someone running down the hall and peeked her head out the door to investigate.

"Who was it?" asked Emily.

"It's that adjunct Bridgette. She ran into the ladies' room. She looks upset. Do you want me to check on her?"

"She's a big girl." Emily paused. "But if it makes you feel better, go ahead."

Susan opened the restroom door and found Bridgette crying at the sink.

"What's wrong? Can I help?" asked Susan.

Sniffling, Bridgette said, "No one can help. It's complicated."

"School trouble? Boyfriend trouble?"

"A little of both. Everything. I'll be fine. I just need some time alone." Bridgette washed her face, and Susan returned to Martha's office.

"Is she okay?" asked Emily.

"She's pretty upset about something but didn't want to talk about it. Like you said, she's a big girl. Should I go through the desk now?" Emily nodded, and Susan took a fresh box to pack up the desk. She found the usual office supplies—staples, paperclips—and personal items such as makeup and a sewing kit. "Hey, here's a card. It says, "From Keith with love.""

"Keith? Maybe that was her boyfriend."

Susan found a letter in the desk, also from Keith. "Hey, this one's X-rated. It has to be her boyfriend."

"Too bad there isn't a last name."

"Wait. She has a cell phone in here. Didn't the police find one in her purse? It must be a secondary one. I'm going to listen to her voice mail. It's not even password protected." She played the first voice mail:

"I'm sorry, what else can I say? If I could take it back, I would. You can't go to my wife. We have to talk. I'll stop by later."

"Whose wife?" asked Susan.

"You've got me," said Emily. "It sounds like Martha found out her boyfriend, Keith, was married."

"To who? Any ideas?"

"We can list the circles I think Martha was in. She was pretty involved with her church; I tagged along once or twice. She sang in the choir. We can nose around there. And there's here. I have a faculty roster. We can look for someone named Keith."

"We should call Martha's sister and see if she ever heard Martha talk about a Keith. She's still at the inn, right? I'd say it's lunch time, my stomach is growling."

"Let's go."

When they arrived at the inn, Coralee greeted them in the lobby, understandably lacking her usual energy and upbeat manner. Susan noted the dark circles under her eyes and her slumped posture. She couldn't imagine having a child arrested, especially as a single parent. Coralee was holding the business together singlehandedly now that Noah was in jail.

"I called the lawyer you recommended, Emily. Had to take out an equity loan to afford his fees, but I have faith he can get the best deal possible for Noah."

Emily said, "Henry loves to work with his hands, and he's pretty good at fixing things. If you need help, don't hesitate to ask. And now that I'm semi-retired, I wouldn't mind helping out with the weekend meal rush."

"You're a great cook, but I couldn't ask you to do that. A teacher from St. Edwards came by looking for part-time work. I think I can swing it. You may know her—Sarah Kimberly."

"Yes, she's a part-time adjunct in the English Department. She was working with Martha, now she's working with Joe Sommers. That's a great idea."

"Come, sit. I'll bring you some menus."

"Thanks, Coralee. You know, we were hoping to talk to Martha's sister. She's still here, isn't she? Maybe she could even join us for lunch."

"Yes. I can call her if you'd like."

While Coralee called, Susan and Emily perused the menu. Susan eyed the garden quiche and decided to order it with a cup of tomato soup. Emily opted for pasta primavera.

"There's Martha's sister now," said Susan. Coralee brought the woman to their table. "I'm glad you could join us. We went through Martha's office and found a voice message from someone named Keith. Do you think he was her boyfriend, and do you know his last name?"

"Now that you mention it, I do remember the name Keith," said the sister. "I don't think she ever said a last name. Do you think he killed her?"

"It wouldn't hurt to talk to him, just to be sure. We'll tell the police," said Emily.

"After we have our apple pie," said Susan.

When they'd finished dessert, Susan and Emily dropped by the police station where they found Detective O'Leary at the front counter.

Emily gave her Martha's cell phone. "We found this in Martha Peterson's desk in her office. Check the phone messages."

Detective O'Leary turned it over in her hand, then held it closer to her eye. "There may have been prints on here. Not anymore since you handled it." She listened to the messages. "Someone named Keith. So? Keith who? And I'm not connecting the dots between the message and him being the killer."

"We heard they argued at the inn the night before Martha's murder, and it sounds like she just found out he was married. You should talk to him," said Susan.

"I don't need advice on how to do my job, ma'am," said the Detective. "It's not enough to go on. We don't have the manpower to search for a needle in a haystack that most likely had nothing to do with the murder. I have to get back to work. Is there anything else?"

"No. Thanks for your time. Come on, Susan. Let's do some shopping."

As soon as they were out of the building, Emily suggested checking the faculty roster. In the parking lot outside her office, they passed Joe Sommers going to his car.

"Hello, ladies. Brrr, the temperature is dropping. I heard on the news we may be in for a snowstorm."

"If you buttoned up that coat of yours and tied your scarf, you'd be warmer," said Emily.

"And perhaps some boots rather than Nikes," added Susan.

He pulled the scarf tighter. "I've got to remember to replace this top button. Have a good afternoon, and try to stay warm."

Once inside Emily's office, they flipped through the faculty roster, which was alphabetical by last name.

"This is frustrating," said Susan. "It's going to take us all day."

They continued going down the list. After a while, Emily said, "Okay, I found two. Keith Phillips over in the Chemistry department and Keith Wilkerson in Economics. Should we take a walk?"

"You bet," said Susan.

The Chemistry department was located across the campus. In spite of the dropping temperature, Susan suggested walking to burn off the calories they'd consumed at lunch. When they found Keith Phillips's office, she said, "It's locked, but here's his class schedule on the door." She rearranged her bifocals. "He's teaching a lecture class right now. Do you know where his room is?"

"It's the big lecture hall downstairs. Let's go." Emily led Susan down the stairs. The wooden doors to the hall were closed. "I don't want to barge in. Let's see if I can do this discreetly." She slowly opened the door, hoping it wouldn't creak and draw attention to them.

When she'd pried it open a few inches, she peeked inside.

Emily whispered, "Well? Can you see anything?"

"This Keith appears to be about eighty. I think we can cross him off the list."

"Darn it."

"We still have one more to go," said Susan. "Where's the Economics Department?"

"It's on the other side of the student union building. Follow me."

Snow fell from the gray sky. When they passed the student union building, Emily said, "In the warmer weather this courtyard is full of students. On days like this, they huddle at the crowded tables inside." Once they turned the corner, Emily pointed out the economics building and led Susan inside. "Let's take the elevator. His office is on the third floor."

All at once, students poured out of classroom doors. Emily looked at her watch and said, "Class just ended. Hopefully, Keith Wilkerson is on his way to his office."

When they arrived at his office, it was locked. Emily said, "Let's give him a few minutes."

Two students came by while they were waiting but left after they tried the door and found it was locked.

"It's been fifteen minutes. Maybe he went right home, trying to beat the bad weather."

Emily said, "Wait. There are two men coming down the hall."

Both men were neatly dressed in jackets and ties. One held a leather briefcase. As they approached, they were laughing, and one put his arm around the other, giving him a quick peck on the cheek. The one with the briefcase said, "Can I help you?"

"We're looking for Keith Wilkerson," said Emily.

"You found him. What can I do for you?"

"I'm a friend of Martha Peterson's, the professor who was murdered. I worked down the hall from her."

"Martha Peterson, how tragic. I can't believe a murder happened right here on campus. Her poor family."

"Did you know Martha?"

"Not personally. Some of my students had her and loved her. How awful. What has our society come to?"

"I know, it's terrible. We were looking for someone who knew her. I think we got the wrong Keith."

"Sorry I couldn't help you." He fumbled with his keys. "I'm going to put this inside and head home with my hubby before the roads get bad. You should do the same. They're predicting quite a storm."

On the way back to the car, Susan said, "At least we eliminated the two Keiths on the faculty. What now?"

"Church. I went with her a few times. She sang in the choir, had rehearsals on Wednesday nights."

"It's Wednesday," said Susan.

"And I happen to know at least one of us can sing." replied Emily with a grin.

Chapter 20

Emily prepared another delicious dinner—chicken cordon bleu with scalloped potatoes and glazed carrots. Susan wondered if was too late to learn how to cook at her age. She had never felt the time it took to prepare food was worth the effort. A delicious meal that takes hours to prepare is generally consumed in under fifteen minutes. And then there was the cleanup. After eating Emily's cooking, however, she was beginning to change her mind.

Henry said, "Did you go through Martha's office?"

"Yes, and we found something very interesting," said Emily. "We found a card to Martha from someone named Keith. The content of it convinced us he was the boyfriend her sister mentioned. Martha's sister didn't have a last name for him. Then we heard a message on her secret cell phone that was in the back of her desk drawer. Keith begged her not to tell his wife about them. That's motive for murder right there. We took the phone to Detective O'Leary, but she wasn't impressed with the new information."

"Emily, don't get carried away," said Henry. Not long ago you made a strong case for Peter Taglieri being the killer. Again, just because someone is guilty of cheating, or for that matter, stealing jewelry, it doesn't make him a murderer."

"I know, but you have to admit it's worth talking to him."

"If we can find him," added Susan. "There are no viable options named Keith on the faculty. We're hoping we'll find him tonight."

"Tonight?" said Mike.

"Yes. Emily says Martha was pretty involved in her church and sang in the choir. They have choir practice tonight."

"Yeah, that makes sense. Find a cheater and possibly a murderer at choir practice. You girls might as well stay home and play Scrabble with us. Besides, aren't the roads supposed to get bad?"

"It wasn't bad coming home," said Emily.

"And you two are just going to waltz right into choir practice. Won't that set off alarms?"

"You know how Martha was always trying to get me to join the choir. They're always happy to add new voices. And Susan was a music teacher. She can really sing."

"If nothing else, it will be fun," said Susan. Mike shook his head in defeat.

After clearing the table and loading the dishwasher, Emily and Susan headed to choir practice, in spite of Henry and Mike's protests. The snow had stopped, and the roads were clear. The white wooden church looked like the model for a postcard.

"What a pretty church," said Susan. "Looks like they have a good turnout judging by this parking lot."

"Come on. I'll introduce you to the pastor. He sings bass—loud and off-key, but he's so enthusiastic no one seems to mind. At least that's what Martha told me."

A middle-aged gentleman with a big smile greeted them. "Emily, right? You came to church with Martha Peterson on a few occasions. We really miss Martha."

Emily said, "I'm surprised you remember me. This is my friend, Susan Wiles. She's visiting from New York. And guess what? She's a retired music teacher.

Thought it would be fun to bring her here tonight. Martha said you are always happy to have new voices."

"How wonderful. Welcome, Susan. Are you an alto or a soprano?"

"Alto," answered Susan.

"And you, Emily?" Emily squirmed, and Susan realized she had no clue what voice part she was. "She's also an alto."

The pastor brought them to the alto section, then took a seat amongst the basses. The choir director, a skinny young man with Harry Potter glasses tapped his baton on the music stand. "Let's start with our warm-ups."

Emily whispered, "What are warm-ups?"

"You'll catch on to the pattern." She remembered hearing Emily sing along to the car radio. "On second thought, just move your lips and look confident."

"There must be at least thirty people here. How are we going to find out if there's a Keith?"

"More than half of them are women, so that narrows it down. I'm working on it."

The choir sang through their hymns, including a four-part rendition of *A Mighty Fortress is our God.* Susan realized how much she missed having music in her life. It was so much fun to be singing again. While singing, she scanned the bass and tenor sections. Many were on the elderly side. She focused on three possibilities, all men who looked to be around Martha's age.

"My mouth is starting to hurt," said Emily. "Maybe this wasn't such a hot idea."

The choir director announced that it was break time. A pot of coffee had been set up in the back of the church.

"Let's mingle," said Susan. "Listen, and maybe we'll hear someone call Keith by name."

"We don't even know Keith is here. Or even if there's a Keith here, that he's the one we're looking for. The guys were right, this is crazy."

"We're here now, so let's give it a shot."

Emily and Susan worked their way around the choir members. Soon the choir director called them back to practice. After another hour of singing, they were no closer to finding Keith.

"This is a dead end," said Emily. "Practice is over. Let's go home." They walked toward the parking lot.

"Keith!" shouted the pastor. Emily and Susan turned around. A rugged-looking man with a gray beard also turned around. "Will you have the programs ready for Sunday?"

"Already done," responded the man. "They're stacked on the counter at my print shop."

"Print shop?" whispered Susan.

"There's only one print shop in town. Guess we're doing some stationary shopping in the morning."

Chapter 21

The next morning over breakfast, Emily announced their plans to go to the print shop.

"You and Mike are welcome to come with us," said Emily.

"Emily," said her husband, "we've hardly spent time all together since our guests arrived. Why don't we go for a hike instead? It's supposed to be a beautiful day according to the weatherman."

"A hike sounds like fun," Emily replied. "After we check out the print shop. It won't take long at all, I promise."

Emily and Susan hurried to get ready and go over to the print shop so they'd have time to pack a picnic lunch before the hike. They parked right in front of the shop and immediately noticed a sign that read "Under New Management. Grand Opening Sale." Only one other customer was in the shop.

"Well, look at that. Peter Taglieri."

"What's he doing here?" whispered Susan.

"Let's go find out. Come on." The two women walked into the shop where they were greeted by Keith. "One minute, and I'll be right with you."

Peter Taglieri grinned at them. "You've seen the light and are ordering *for-sale* posters for your house, right?"

Susan wished she could take a stack of envelopes and stuff them down his throat. He took such pleasure in harassing her friend. Good thing Emily had thick skin.

Peter picked up a stack of flyers from the counter. "Thanks, Keith. I'm going to send these out ASAP. Glad you took over this place. You're much quicker than the previous owner." He held one up for the girls to see. "I'm sending these advertisements down to Florida. It will be brutally hot there soon, and with all those retirees… tiny, cheap houses in a cool climate will attract them like ants to honey, just watch. And wait till the residents here see the income possibilities once that starts to happen. I won't be the only one pressuring you to sell." He left the shop, shooting them another grin on his way out the door.

Keith said, "Sorry for the wait. What can I help you with?"

"I'm Emily Fox. I teach at St. Edwards College. Martha Peterson was a friend and colleague."

"I think I saw you at choir practice last night. Sorry, but I don't know a Martha Peterson."

"She sang in the choir, went to your church. You must have known her. Reddish hair, about my age and height?"

Keith twirled the gold band on his finger. "Um, yeah. Now I remember."

"Look, I'm just going to be direct with you. Martha was a friend, and I will find out who killed her if the police don't find out first. I know you were seeing Martha. We found a letter and a phone message from you to her."

Susan noticed sweat beading on his face. I think he's falling for Emily's bluff.

"The police will be much easier on you if you come forward on your own," Susan said. "I know that because my daughter is a detective back home. You could plead manslaughter or self-defense if it applies. In any case, if you cooperate, things will be easier for you."

"Cooperate! I'm no murderer. I didn't kill Martha, I loved her."

"So you *were* involved with Martha. Then she found out you were married and threatened to tell your wife. You couldn't let that happen."

"What? Are you crazy? Look, Martha did threaten to tell my wife. At first I was very upset. I may have even made a threat or two. But then I came clean with my wife after talking to Pastor Bob. I apologized to Martha, made a clean break. By the way, Martha wasn't happy with me. We had a terrible argument last time we were together, but I certainly didn't kill her. My wife and I have been attending marriage counseling at the church. Things are good. Better than ever in fact."

"Can you prove it?"

"If you went through her phone messages, I hope you checked her texts also. There you'll find my apology for the previous threats. And you can check with Pastor Bob. He knows what happened and certainly is a credible source."

Another customer came through the door. "If you'll excuse me, I have to work. Send the police over. I'll tell them everything I just told you."

Emily and Susan got into the Jeep. "Sounds like we eliminated him," said Susan.

"It does. Let's stop by the police station and tip them off about looking for a phone text. Keith, Noah, and Sarah Kimberly were the three we thought had motive to kill Martha. Sarah was seen on the recording of the inauguration, so she has an alibi. It looks like Keith checks out."

"So either Noah tried to kill her to prevent her going to the police about him stealing…"

"Or the murderer was one hundred percent after me," said Emily.

"Let's stop at the station, then pick up sandwich fixings for our hike," said Susan.

When they arrived, both Detective Wooster and Detective O'Leary were available. *I hope this is worth our time,* thought Susan. *Last time we came here we were treated like a pair of interfering amateurs.*

"Back so soon?" said Detective O'Leary. Emily and Susan flashed her a smile.

Detective Wooster ushered them into his office, and Emily explained what they had learned from talking to Keith at the print shop.

"Mrs. Fox," explained Wooster, "we did our job. We went through the phone messages, then checked the text messages. We saw that Keith apologized to Mrs. Peterson. We talked to Keith's wife to establish an alibi, and he had one. The two of them were at a counseling session during the time of the murder."

"You verified that?" said Susan.

Detective Wooster gave her a look and took a breath. "Yes, Mrs. Wiles. Of course we verified it. Now stay out of this investigation and go enjoy your vacation."

An officer knocked on the door. "Detective, I got the information you requested. The suspect has an alibi. He was committing a robbery at the inn at the time of the murder. A guest reported taking a shower, and her necklace was gone when she came out. It was a ten-minute window."

"Noah has an alibi," said Susan. "That's great news. Come on, Emily. Let's go tell Coralee."

"That's not for you to tell," said Detective Wooster. "This is police business. It's up to us to tell Coralee Saunders that her son has an alibi for the time of Martha Peterson's murder because at the time, he was busy stealing jewelry from one of her guests. Now, if you'll excuse us, we have work to do."

Emily and Susan exited the station. Susan said, "All our suspects with motives to kill Martha are cleared."

"Great," replied Emily. "All that means is that *I* was the one who was supposed to die that day. Martha died because of me. That guilt will haunt me forever. Noah is in the clear. We're back to Peter Taglieri as our prime suspect."

"Hey, let's stop by the inn," Susan suggested. "I saw a sign on the front desk about ordering box lunches. Let's pick up four of those, then meet the guys for our hike. And while we're there, it might just slip out that Noah is cleared."

"That will be a relief to Coralee."

Emily called Henry from the car to tell him they were picking up lunches and to be ready to go on the hike as soon as they got home. When they arrived at the inn, Coralee greeted them in the lobby.

"Coralee, we came to pick up some of those famous box lunches. We're going hiking this afternoon."

"I'm glad to see you're finally getting in some fun with your friends."

"How are things going with Noah?"

"The lawyer has it under control. At least the burglary charges. I don't know what to think about the murder accusations."

Susan couldn't resist. "We happened to be the police station when they verified Noah was stealing a necklace at the time of Martha's murder. He has an alibi. He's off the hook."

"Really? That's good news. My son was stealing a necklace from one of my guests, so he has an alibi for Martha's murder. But the police are also trying to implicate him in that girl's disappearance ten years ago. Noah swears he didn't have anything to do with it and I believe him. He was all of sixteen years old at the time."

"They don't have any physical evidence," said Susan. "All they have is Ashley's car hidden in a barn. How old did you say he was? Sixteen? I'll bet he wasn't even driving then."

"He was," replied Coralee, "but, hey, that's when he had his foot surgery. He'd gotten his permit, but right afterward he had foot surgery. He messed up his right ankle playing soccer. Had two different surgeries that year. He couldn't have killed Ashley. The college took him off yard work and had him working in the admissions office for months."

"Really? Foot surgery?" said Susan. "Then he couldn't have driven Ashley's car all the way to the barn, right? Get the medical records down to the police station right now."

Coralee threw her arms around Susan.

Chapter 22

Henry parked the Jeep and slung the backpack with their lunches over his shoulder. The winding, mountain road ended in a large gravel parking lot, surrounded by picnic tables and pavilions. In spite of the cold weather, several tables were occupied. Emily spread out a checkered tablecloth that she kept in the trunk of her car, and they dined on gourmet sandwiches, German-style potato salad, and grapes. The trails were marked according to level of difficulty. Henry suggested the yellow trail, which was somewhere between easy and challenging.

"This takes us past the waterfall. The view from the turnaround is spectacular."

They followed Henry up the dirt trail, passing a few hikers along the way. Susan saw a familiar face. Joe Sommers and Bridgette, were hiking back toward the parking lot. *I know Emily doesn't think there's anything going on,* she thought, *but why is Joe hanging out with this young adjunct?*

"Emily and gang," said Joe. "Nice day to be outside."

"I see you brought Bridgette along," said Susan.

"We're discussing her dissertation. Just as easy to do it here as stuck inside."

Looks to me like Bridgette would be more comfortable in his office, Susan thought. *She's stiff and certainly isn't smiling. She looks like she's yearning to be anywhere but here.*

"As long as the work gets done, right?" added Emily.

"Speaking of work, are you reinterviewing your sources for the book?" Joe asked.

"Yes," Emily replied. "As a matter of fact, I'm talking to a source tomorrow who remembered some new information. I'm hoping it will move things along."

"New information? After ten years?" said Joe.

"Hopefully it will be a lead. We'd better keep moving," Emily said.

"Good luck," said Joe. "Susan and Mike, you're in for a treat. The view from the top of the trail is breathtaking. It's so clear you can see for miles. We've gotta get going too. I'll see you tomorrow, Emily." Joe and Bridgette disappeared down the path.

When they were out of earshot, Susan said, "Emily, do you think Joe is acting professionally, taking that adjunct out on a hike like that? And he took her to dinner the other day. She doesn't look comfortable with him."

"Joe's a bit of a nonconformist. He'll do pretty much anything to get out of doing work. I'm sure it's fine."

"Now that it seems Noah is in the clear, are you going to reinterview some of your sources for the book?" Susan asked. "I heard you tell Joe you had a lead,"

"Most definitely. Ashley had a close friend who still lives in the area. When I first interviewed her, she mentioned someone bothering—actually she used the word harassing—her. She couldn't remember more details back then. I'm planning on talking to her tomorrow. Want to tag along?"

"Of course," said Susan.

"Look at that scenery," said Mike. "Come on, pose for a picture." Mike snapped a photo of his three friends at the summit. After soaking up the view, they turned around and continued on the path back to the car. Along the way, Susan picked up a few smooth stones to bring back for Annalise. Annalise loved the outdoors, and Lynnette had helped her daughter set up a collection of shells, dried leaves, pressed wildflowers, and rocks.

"The college is hosting a community arts fair tonight. Want to go?" said Emily.

"I'd love that," said Susan. Mike and Henry agreed. They piled into the car for the trip home.

When Henry pulled the Jeep into the driveway, Susan felt an unexplainable chill run up her spine. *Something isn't right*, she thought. As they approached the front door, Emily screamed, "Hurry, Henry. Unlock the door. Look, the window is broken."

Mike grabbed his wife's forearm and said to Emily, "Call the police first. Someone could be inside."

"I'm on it. Mike's right. Stay outside." Henry pulled out his cell phone and called Detective Wooster.

"Come on, I don't want to wait," said Emily. "I want to see what's missing." She cautiously opened the door, brushing past Henry. Dusk had fallen, and she couldn't see. She tiptoed toward the lamp when suddenly something jumped toward her. She let out another scream. Susan froze and followed suit, screaming even louder than Emily had.

Emily caught her breath. Susan's heart stopped thumping. "Chester! Don't scare us like that." The cat ran off and hid under the loft ladder. Emily checked the kitchen, the bedroom, and then climbed up to the loft and rummaged through the dresser drawers. When she came back downstairs, she said. "Nothing seems to be missing."

"What's this?" Henry picked up a large rock. "This is how they broke in."

"What's that taped to it?" said Susan.

Henry pulled the paper from the rock. "It's a note."

Emily read it over his shoulder. "Let sleeping dogs lie."

"What does that mean?" said Susan.

"Obviously it's a threat," said Henry. He put his hands on his wife's shoulders. "Someone doesn't want you to continue writing your book. Maybe you should pay attention. It's not worth putting your life in danger."

Susan, nerves still primed, jumped when Detective Wooster pushed through the partially opened door. "Is everyone okay?"

"We're fine. This was thrown through the window." Henry handed him the rock and the note. The detective warned the group to stay put while he searched the house.

We shouldn't have ignored the possibility that someone may have been hiding in the house when Henry brought it up, Susan thought. *If Emily had gone into the bedroom and someone had been hiding in there...*

"All clear," announced the detective. "Is anything missing?"

"Doesn't seem to be. My laptop and television are still here," said Emily. "I searched the bedroom. Jewelry is all there. I had some expensive pieces sitting right out on the dresser."

"Clearly robbery wasn't the motive. We'll check for fingerprints and talk to the neighbors; see if anyone saw anything. I've got a squad car on the way."

Kurt Olav came through the door, startling Susan. "What's going on? I saw the police car. Are you okay?"

"Someone threw a rock through the window and left a threatening note. Did you see anyone?" Henry asked.

"No, Henry. I was in town. Just got back myself." He looked at the window. "I'll help you fix that. Where's your broom?"

"We'll replace the glass tomorrow. For tonight, help me cover it over with plywood."

The detective came back into the house. "Buzz next door thinks he heard a car drive past about an hour or two ago. Didn't see anyone. He asked if word was going to get around. Something about bad publicity, crime in the area bringing down housing values."

"They want us to sell our place to Peter Taglieri," said Emily, "so he can make a tiny house community. Taglieri offered us both a ton of money, but we aren't going anywhere."

"Like my wife said," Henry added, "they want us to sell. Do you think it was them trying to scare us away?"

"Peewee and the tiny houses community," said Wooster. "He's persistent all right, but if he's trying to avoid bad publicity, I'd think no. And does the note make sense in that scenario?"

"Only if he wants me to stop writing my book and bringing up the Ashley Young disappearance."

"Board up that window and keep the house locked up tight," the Detective ordered. "I'll let you know if we get any prints. Meanwhile, if you think of anything else, call the station."

Chapter 23

The next day, the glass had been swept clean, and the boarded-up window blocked the morning light. After breakfast, Susan and Emily drove to see Ashley's old friend, Karen Roberts. Karen lived on the other side of the lake with her husband and daughter. When they pulled into the driveway, a snow-covered swing set was visible off to the side of the house. The front yard was full of bare trees with icy branches.

"Come on in, Mrs. Fox." Karen Roberts was in her thirties. She wore jeans and a Patriots sweatshirt.

"Thanks for agreeing to sit down with me again. This is my friend, Susan Wiles. Someone is going to some lengths to prevent me from writing this book, Karen, which means I'm more convinced than ever of foul play. You know, they found Ashley's car, so that pretty much rules out a voluntary disappearance."

"That should have been ruled out ten years ago. Voluntary disappearance? Ashley never would have left like that. She would have told me and her parents if she was planning on leaving."

A little girl in pink overalls came into the room, whining for a snack.

"She's adorable," said Susan. "How old?"

"She just turned four. I can't imagine how Ashley's parents feel being without their daughter and not knowing what happened to her. I hope you stir up enough interest with your book that the police will reopen the investigation."

Karen excused herself to fix her daughter a snack and emerged from the kitchen with a plate of cookies. *Everywhere we go we've been offered coffee and homemade baked goods,* Susan thought. *That's something you don't see back in New York.*

Susan said, "You know, I have a granddaughter who's a little younger than yours. Children are such a blessing."

"A handful at times but most definitely a blessing."

"These are delicious, Karen. Now, you said you remembered something." Emily wiped the crumbs from her mouth.

"Yes. I told you Ashley mentioned something about being harassed. I think he wasn't local. She said he was trying to get her to go back with him to meet his parents. He said he'd pay for the plane ticket, so it must not have been close to here. Oh, and something else. We had another friend who moved away, but I ran into her at the store the other day. She's living here now. Maybe she'd be worth talking to."

"Great. What's her name?"

"I don't know her married name, but her first name is pretty unusual. It's Kiki."

After the two women left, Emily told Susan that she couldn't believe her very own neighbor had been friends with Ashley Young. Neither could Susan. She wondered if the two had been friends, why doesn't Kiki want to learn what happened? Instead, she's trying to prevent the case from being reopened.

"Do you think Kiki knows what happened?" said Susan.

"There's one way to find out. Let's stop by their place on the way home."

When they got back to Maplewood, both Kiki and Buzz's cars were in the driveway.

Kiki answered the door wearing tight leather pants and a silk shirt.

"What are you doing here? Decide to sell yet?"

"No," said Emily. "I came to talk to you about Ashley Young. I understand the two of you were friends."

"So? It doesn't mean I want you stirring up bad publicity. It's history now. I don't have any information for you."

Still standing in the doorway, Emily said, "Just tell us if there's anyone at all you think could have harmed her. The sooner the case is solved, the quicker Sugerbury Falls goes back to being a safe little town. If a killer is still lurking out here…"

"Okay, okay," replied Kiki. "I remember she said something about a creepy, old professor giving her a hard time. That's all I know. And that boy, Noah Saunders. He had a huge crush on her. She said he was coming on pretty strong. A few times we saw him on the way out of class, and she asked me to walk her to her car."

Buzz, carrying a beer, appeared and put his arm around Kiki. "What're you talking to this holdout for? She's not welcome here." He let out a noisy burp.

"It's okay. We were just leaving." Emily got out of the door with Susan seconds before Buzz slammed it closed.

What a jerk. The sooner they move back to the city the better, Susan thought.

Emily rolled down the window and grabbed the mail from the mailbox at the end of the driveway. "What timing. It's Ashley's transcript. Came sooner than expected."

As soon as the women got inside, Emily tore open the letter. "She had five professors that semester. Two were women. The English professor I don't know. He must have left before I started. The others we can look into."

"So three men."

"Including the one who left. If he was involved, that could be why he left. Tomorrow we'll go over to the campus and ask around."

When they got up to the house, the men, with Kurt Olav's help, were in the process of repairing the window. Kurt and Mike lifted the newly cut glass into the frame.

"Guess what?" said Emily. "Turns out Kiki went to school here and was friends with Ashley. She told us Ashley was being bothered by a creepy professor—to use her own words—and Noah Saunders, who we now know is innocent."

"I'm surprised she was willing to give you any help at all," said Henry. "That's the second reference to a professor or being worried about a grade."

Emily waved the envelope. "And now I've got Ashley's transcript. We can start investigating her professors."

"Or the police can," said Henry.

Kurt wiped his brow. "I need some sandpaper. Do you have some?"

"Not in here," said Henry, pointing to his toolbox. "There are some random odds and ends in the barn. Here, take the key."

Henry picked up the tools while Mike stirred a can of paint. A few minutes later, Kurt returned from the barn with the sandpaper.

"Here's the key," he said to Henry. "You know it was unlocked, don't you?"

"Unlocked? No way would I have left it unlocked."

"I locked it back up," said Kurt. "After last time…"

"I find it highly unlikely another thief is storing loot in there, but thanks for doing me the favor," said Henry.

"It's too bad we missed the exhibit last night," said Susan.

Emily said, "No, we didn't. It's going on tonight also. How about dinner at the inn and we go to the campus afterward?"

"I think we've got a plan," said Henry.

Chapter 24

The inn parking lot was full when they arrived at Coralee's. They had to wait a few minutes for a table. Coralee came through the lobby, hair mussed and eyes drooping.

"Coralee, what's wrong?" said Emily.

"I don't know if I can talk about it. It's too upsetting."

"You can tell us."

Coralee led them into the alcove. "I found something in Noah's closet. It was crumpled in the back like he was hiding it."

"What is it?" asked Susan. "Noah has been cleared of the murder charge and is in jail for stealing, so how bad could it be?"

"Come on, Emily. Follow me."

All four followed Coralee upstairs to Noah's room. Coralee reached into the back of the closet. "Here."

Emily took the item. Her mouth fell open. "It's a red scarf."

"Unfold it. Look."

"Oh, Coralee. I see why you're upset."

Susan said, "Let me see."

"It's a scarf with initials sewn into it. The initials are *AY*. Ashley Young. Why does Noah have Ashley's scarf, ten years later, hidden in his closet?"

"It looks dirty, like it was dragged on the ground or run over by a car."

"Yes, Susan. Maybe Ashley was wearing it when Noah knocked her out and dragged her on the ground. Or worse." Coralee covered her face with her hands.

Henry said, "You said he had a broken ankle, had just had surgery, right?"

"Yes."

"There's no way he could have dragged more than a hundred pounds of dead weight anywhere. He wouldn't have had the balance."

Coralee sunk onto the bed. "You're right. But why was it in his closet?"

"I think you need to visit the jail and ask him," said Henry.

"I was able to meet his bail. He'll be coming home tomorrow."

Emily hugged her. "That's great news."

Clearing his throat, Henry said, "Meanwhile, can a guy get something to eat around here?"

"I'm sorry, Henry."

"Coralee, I was just trying to lighten the mood," said Henry. "Take time to compose yourself. Our table should be ready, and I saw more than one server down there."

The foursome entered the dining room, which had cleared out a bit. Susan was glad to see Coralee could afford to keep on help as well as meet Noah's bail. Emily said she'd probably had to take out a second mortgage in order to do so.

"I'm having prime rib, fried onions, and crème brulee," said Mike. He smiled at Susan. "Just kidding. Baked chicken breast, broccoli, and steamed rice."

The girls ordered pasta Bolognese, while Henry enjoyed a filet mignon. After dinner, they drove to St. Edwards where the arts fair was in full swing. The student union building was set up with rows of tables displaying artwork, poems, short stories, and musical compositions. In one corner, a renaissance group played madrigals on original instruments. The theater department ran a series of one-act plays in the auditorium, and a string quartet played Mozart sonatas in the lobby.

"This is incredible," said Susan. "The quartet sounds great."

"And look at these paintings," said Mike.

They strolled through the aisles, admiring the student work. Sarah Kimberly, who was reading a short story at one of the tables, looked up when she saw Emily.

"Some great work here, Sarah. Didn't you submit some poems too?"

"I did. They're on the next table." Sarah fidgeted and opened her mouth to speak twice, seeming to change her mind before words came out.

"Are you okay, Sarah?" Emily asked. "You look like you want to tell me something."

"It's... It's just... Can I come by your office tomorrow? I need to talk to you about something confidential."

"Of course. Stop by after my morning class."

After Sarah walked away, Emily said, "I wonder what that's about?"

"I guess you'll find out tomorrow," replied Susan.

Several of Emily's colleagues and students stopped to chat and meet Susan and Mike. Joe Sommers passed them as they were leaving.

"What a wonderful feast of talent," said Joe. "Several of my students have work displayed."

"I love the music," said Susan. "Those authentic renaissance instruments are a bear to play."

"Joe, we have a copy of Ashley Young's transcript from the semester she went missing." Emily pulled the paper from her purse. "Do you know any of these professors?"

Joe looked at the list. "I know Dr. Johnson from the math department. She and I were on a committee together."

"How about the three men? One was an English professor. He was in our department."

"I vaguely remember him. He had some problems. Drinking I think. He took a leave part way through the year if I remember correctly."

"What about Ashley Young? Did you know her?"

"No, not personally. Of course, everyone knew her name. The case was high profile, but you know that. Took some time to die down. I guess your book will be bringing it to the forefront once again. Have you found any new evidence?"

"Nah. Not yet."

Susan respected the fact that Emily kept the information about the scarf to herself. She knew that rumors fly fast and furious, especially in a small town.

"Emily, I left something in my office. Can I borrow my spare key from you?" Joe asked.

Emily took it off her key chain. "It was a good idea giving each other copies. This isn't the first time we've needed them."

"I'll give it back tomorrow. Have a good evening."

When they got back to the house, Emily made coffee while the others got comfortable in the living room. Henry turned on the late news.

"Oh my God," said Henry. "Look. Emily, come in here." He turned up the volume. "They found a grave. It's right behind Peewee Miniatures."

"Did they find a skeleton? Is it Ashley Young?" Susan stepped closer to the screen and adjusted her bifocals.

"They say it's empty," said Mike.

"No, look. They found something." Susan pointed to the screen. The camera went to a close-up. Henry turned the volume higher. "It's a tassel. From a ski hat."

Emily said, "Not just a tassel. A red tassel."

"Red. Like the scarf in Noah's closet," said Susan.

Chapter 25

The next morning, Susan sat in the back of the classroom and watched her friend teach. She had to admit that as much as she had loved teaching, she was happy to no longer have the responsibility it entailed. Getting acclimated to the retirement lifestyle had taken a little time, but she was grateful she now had control over her own schedule, more time to spend with her family, and time to enjoy her favorite pastime—solving mysteries. The puzzle of crime solving kept her brain young in the way they said yoga would keep her body young. She wasn't convinced about the yoga, given it was taking her longer and longer to get out of cushioned, low-to-the-ground furniture.

At the end of class, Emily asked some of the students to stay. She had a list of the three professors from Ashley's transcript and showed it to them.

"This professor is no longer here, but do any of you know these two?"

One girl jumped in. "I had Dr. Mathers for two different courses. He's great. Everyone loves him."

Another girl said, "I had him too. Very professional, very organized."

"Did he ever mingle with his students after class?"

"No, he had office hours, but other than that he didn't hang around campus much."

"Thanks, girls. Do you know this one? Dr. Smith?"

"No, never had him." Both girls shook their heads, gathered their backpacks, and left.

Susan said, "Sounds like Dr. Mathers wasn't the type we're looking for, but we should run by and talk to him. Dr. Smith too."

Emily led the way. Dr. Mathers was in the next building. He had just finished teaching a class when they found his office. He was an older gentleman, bald, Santa Claus stomach.

"Can I help you?"

"I work in the next building. I've seen you in the parking lot a few times."

"Yes, you look familiar. Come into my office. Who's your friend?"

"Susan Wiles. A dear friend visiting from New York. I teach here, but I'm also a writer. I'm working on a true crime book about the Ashley Young case and noticed she had been one of your students."

"We all know the name, but I can't say I can place her. The police asked me ten years ago, and I didn't even know who she was back then. She was in one of my large lecture classes. Never came to my office as far as I can remember. Wish I could be more help."

"It's been a long time, and I know what you mean. I can't place all my students with their faces either. Did you happen to know a professor named William Rowan? He taught in the English department."

"We were on a committee together. Quiet man. Had health issues and wound up leaving midsemester."

"Were there any rumors about him going after his female students or anything like that?"

"Heavens, no. That kind of stuff doesn't happen here at St. Edwards. Maybe in some of those city schools like in New York or something but not here."

"Thanks. I'll be seeing you in the parking lot." Both she and Dr. Mathers smiled.

Susan followed Emily outside. They walked across the campus to find Dr. Smith. Susan took one look at him and said, "That isn't our guy. Handsome and too young even now to be referred to as a creepy old man. He probably had just started teaching. He doesn't look forty yet."

"You're right. Let's go by my office and check the 'Rate My Professor' database and see if there were any complaints filed on the other two."

Joe Sommers walked in. "Whatcha doing? You're usually gone by now." He reached into his pocket. "Let me give you back my spare key before I forget."

"Thanks. We're checking into Ashley Young's professors. The only one we don't have info on is the one who left midway through the semester. Did you know William Rowan? He worked in this department."

"Yeah, his office was where Martha's was."

"Did students ever complain about him harassing them or doing anything inappropriate?"

"As a matter of fact, I did hear some gossip from the students back then. He had an eye for the pretty ladies. He was thrown out for drinking on the job."

"Do you know who took over for him and exactly when it was? It's important for my book."

"He was Ashley Young's professor. I even saw him with her a few times from the window. One day they were arguing out in the parking lot. A real screaming match, not long before she died come to think of it."

"Do you know where he went after he left?"

"I think he was going back to his hometown, somewhere in the Midwest. Hope it's helpful."

"Yes, thanks, Joe."

After Joe left, Emily googled William Rowan. "No bad reports from students, no arrest record. Looks like he works out in Ann Arbor. Been there for eight years, so I suppose whatever problems he was having, he managed to overcome them."

"Well, it doesn't mean he wasn't bothering Ashley Young. It's more likely him than the other professors she had."

"What time is Sarah coming by?"

Emily looked at her watch. "She should have been here by now."

They waited almost an hour. Just as they were getting ready to leave, Emily's office phone rang.

"Sarah, Where are you?"

"I… I won't be coming in. It's too dangerous. Sorry I made you wait."

"Sarah. Sarah, where are you?" Emily hung up the phone. "She's not coming. She says she's afraid. She didn't say where she is."

"Afraid? Why don't you call Coralee and see if she showed up for her last shift."

"Better yet, let's stop there on our way home."

On their way out of the building, they passed Bridgette. Emily asked her if she'd seen Sarah.

"Yeah, I saw her about an hour ago. She was in the parking lot. Looked like she was in a hurry. She didn't even respond when I said hello to her."

"Has she been acting like herself lately, other than just now?"

"I'd say so. But I don't really know. She's a teacher. Status quo as far as I could tell."

"Thanks, Bridgette."

"If she was here an hour ago, she intended to talk to me. What spooked her, and why was she too afraid to talk to me?"

"Maybe it isn't what. Maybe it's who."

Chapter 26

On the way home from the campus, Coralee called Emily and asked if she and Susan could stop by.

"Is she alright?" asked Susan.

"She sounds upset. She said she just picked up Noah from the jail."

"I wonder if she asked him about the scarf. The red scarf, which is the same color as the tassel found in the abandoned grave."

Emily pushed the customary speed limit, winding through the road to the inn. "I hope everything is okay."

At the inn, Coralee brought them into the alcove where Noah was seated. He needed a shave but smelled as though he just came out of the shower. Emily gave him a hug.

Coralee said, "I asked Noah about the scarf. He says he found it in your barn!"

"In our barn?" said Emily. "When? And how is that possible?"

Noah said, "I was stealing jewelry and hiding it in the metal box in the horse stall in your barn. Just before I was caught, I walked in and saw the scarf on the ground near the ladder to the loft. It was mostly buried under the dirt, but I saw a bit of bright red and bent down to see what it was. I brushed off the dirt, and that's when I realized it was Ashley's scarf. At least I assumed it was, with her initials embroidered into it and all."

Emily said, "Why didn't you go right to the police? Why on earth did you hide it in your closet?"

"What was I supposed to say? I was hiding stolen jewelry and came across a scarf that belongs to a possible murder victim who has been missing for ten years? They would've thought I did it. I was already breaking the law by stealing."

"You have to go to the police now," said Emily.

"Mom already called them. I just hope it doesn't land me right back in jail."

Susan said, "Ashley's car was found in the Anderson barn, which was recently bought by Peter Taglieri. An empty grave with a red tassel in it was found behind Taglieri's makeshift office. Noah finds a red scarf in your barn. We don't know how long it's been there."

"Henry's parents used the barn when they lived here," said Emily. "They would have noticed the scarf. It had to have been left there during the course of the past year. Noah, remember you had foot surgery right before Ashley went missing. You couldn't have driven her car or dragged her to a grave. Medical records will confirm that."

Detectives Wooster and O'Leary arrived. Noah brought the scarf down from his closet and handed it to them, explaining the circumstances under which he found it.

Detective Wooster said, "The wool and color look like the tassel we found. They are both equally ground with dirt. They certainly don't look new."

"So Ashley's body was buried in a grave, then recently removed and hidden in our barn?" said Emily.

"We haven't confirmed that it's Ashley Young. We are waiting for DNA and blood results."

"Come on," said Susan. "Have you had any other murders here that are unsolved?"

Detective Wooster's phone rang. "Excuse me." He took the call in the next room.

Detective O'Leary said, "We have to have solid evidence before we can make a statement. We'll know soon enough if it's Ashley Young. Meanwhile, we'll process the scarf." She put the scarf into an evidence bag. "Mr. Saunders, we'll need a sample of your DNA. For elimination purposes."

"Sure, whatever I can do to help. I liked Ashley. I hope you find out what really happened to her."

Detective Wooster came back into the alcove. His partner asked about the call.

"It was the lab. There were traces of blood on the tassel, and it's the same type as Ashley Young." He motioned to Detective O'Leary. "Let's go,"

"Coralee, is Sarah Kimberly still working for you?" said Susan. In the commotion about the scarf, they'd forgotten to ask.

"It's funny you mention her. She was supposed to work tonight but called in a little while ago to say she's sick and won't be in. It's gonna leave me shorthanded, but then again, I have Noah back, at least for now."

"Call me if you need anything," said Emily. She and Susan headed home.

"I'm really getting worried. Sarah was upset and scared. She missed our appointment as well as her last shift at the inn. Something's wrong. I feel it."

They passed Kurt Olav walking with someone as they neared the house.

"Who's that young girl he's talking to?" asked Susan. Kurt and the mysterious girl were walking away from the road. Susan strained to see. "The girl is slim and has long blond hair. She looks like Sarah Kimberly from the back, doesn't she?"

Emily, still driving the car, squinted. "It sure does." She rolled down the window and called Kurt's name, but he didn't turn around. "Kurt!"

"He's too far away. I'm sure he can't hear you," said Susan.

"Or he doesn't want to," said Emily. "Why on earth would he be talking to Sarah Kimberly? I didn't think they knew each other."

Once inside, Emily explained to Henry and Mike how the scarf wound up in Noah's closet.

Henry said, "How it wound up in his closet is one thing. How it wound up in our barn is the bigger mystery. Maybe we should give the barn a thorough going through."

"I'm game," said Mike. "Girls? Do I need to ask?"

"No, just let me change out of my work clothes. By the way, we saw Kurt walking with a young blond girl. Henry, have you ever seen him with anyone?"

"Never. The guy's a hermit as far as I know. I think we're his only friends."

Henry grabbed a flashlight, and Susan grabbed a few baggies in case they found evidence. They went out to the barn, and Henry propped open the large doors on the side.

"We need to be methodical," said Susan. "Up and down in a grid pattern. We should move the equipment and the stuff that's in the stalls."

The foursome went to work. Henry and Mike pulled out the equipment. Susan and Emily worked their way through the stalls. Susan was sweating in spite of the freezing temperature.

"I'd have hated to be a farmer," said Susan. "I'm not cut out for physical labor."

"And we've only covered half the barn. It's starting to get dark out."

Henry drove the tractor outside. When he came back in and inspected the area where it had been parked, he said, "Look! Where the tractor was. There's a latch in the floor." He brushed it with his gloved hand. "Hand me that broom." He swept the dirt away and pulled up on the latch. He yanked hard on the handle. "It's not moving."

Emily knelt beside him and felt along the trapdoor. "Give me the shovel." She chipped into the caked dirt and freed the door. "Voilà."

All eyes stared down into the hole. Henry shone the flashlight. The opening wasn't deep, maybe three feet and the width of two refrigerators. For a moment no one dared breathe. Henry gave the flashlight to Emily and ran his hand around the secret compartment. Mike handed him a shovel.

"The bottom is solid. Can't get down any deeper. Nobody's down here, dead or otherwise."

Susan said, "Wait. Look." She pulled out a bit of red yarn and put it in a baggie. "See. Ashley's body was here. It could have been here for years. Henry, did your parents know about the hiding place?"

"I'm sure they didn't. They never mentioned it, and I never saw it in all the summers I spent here."

"Then where is she now?" said Mike.

"And who is playing hide-and-seek with her remains?" said Susan.

Chapter 27

The next morning, Kurt Olav knocked on the door before breakfast. "I saw police cars out at your barn last night. What happened?"

Henry said, "We found a secret compartment in the ground inside the barn. We found evidence Ashley Young may have been buried there. The police are confirming it."

"Really? Remember I saw someone lurking around there even after Noah Saunders was arrested."

And people call me nosy? I'm not half as nosy as this guy, Susan thought.

Emily poured a mug of coffee and handed it to Kurt. "We saw you walking yesterday with a young lady. I called to you from the car, but you must not have heard me."

"A young lady? It sure wasn't me. What young lady would want to hang around with an old geezer like me?"

"It sure looked like you. Even wearing a jacket like yours."

"Coralee gets all kinds of visitors at the inn. Probably some couple taking a scenic hike or something."

Susan, trying to diffuse any defensiveness, said, "A hike is probably right. We had a beautiful hike this afternoon. A picnic too."

"A picnic in February? The sun was pretty strong today. Glad you're enjoying our neck of the woods."

Emily refilled Kurt's coffee and sat down next to him. Chester jumped on her lap. Oftentimes the cat hid when visitors came, but he'd always seemed comfortable around Kurt.

"Kurt, do you happen to know a woman named Sarah Kimberly? She's an adjunct instructor over at the school." As Emily talked, Susan studied Kurt's body language as he answered.

"I'm not the academic sort. Other than you, I don't know anyone over there. Thanks for the coffee." Kurt declined Emily's breakfast invitation.

After he left, Susan said, "I can tell he's hiding something. Did you see how he fidgeted when you asked if he knew Sarah?"

"If it was Sarah, at least we know she's alive and well. I'll try her." Emily called Sarah's cell phone. "She's not answering. I hope she's hiding out somewhere, safe from whomever she's afraid of. I wish she'd reach out to me again."

"Maybe she's at school," said Susan. It's highly doubtful, but at least Emily will feel like we're doing something to find her.

After promising the men that they'd all explore the downtown stores later, Susan and Emily headed to the school. When they opened the front door, Kiki and Buzz zipped past them, then parked their motorcycle— another millennial toy for days when the snow wasn't deep enough for the snowmobile.

Kiki said, "We heard they found a grave inside your barn. You know, that would give me the creeps, knowing I was yards away from a dead body all this time."

Emily said, "If you got your information right, you know that the 'grave' was empty."

"Empty or not, it's still a grave. We're already hearing rumors that the barn is haunted. Sell now. Let

Peter Taglieri demolish the ghost abode." Kiki did her best imitation of a moaning ghost.

"You know, an empty grave was found behind Taglieri's makeshift office. I'll bet he has something to do with this," said Emily.

"Digging up graves, digging up old dirt on Ashley Young's case... Is that what retired people do?" asked Kiki.

Susan held Emily back, sensing she was about to punch Kiki in the face. Emily did have a feisty side to her. "Come on, Emily. Let's go." They jumped into the Jeep. Emily couldn't resist revving the motor and peeling out, leaving Kiki and Buzz in the dust.

"I'm glad we never had kids," said Emily. "Imagine if you got stuck with ones like those two."

"How kids turn out is no accident. I'm sure their parents are every bit as horrible as they are. You and Henry would have done a great job, that's who you are." She saw a tear in Emily's eye. Emily's phone rang. "It's Sarah."

"Ask her if we can meet with her."

"Sarah, I'm with Susan Wiles in the car. Tell us where you are, and we'll be right there."

"No, I can't. I saw something I shouldn't have and I'm scared."

"About Martha's murder?"

"About Ashley's. I gotta go. Someone's following me."

"Sarah, give us more. Let us get the police."

"No. Ashley's dead, and I know who killed her. I have proof."

"Sarah, I'm losing you. You're breaking up. Sarah..."

"What happened? What did she say?"

"I lost the call. The last thing I heard was professor and Midwest. I think that's what she said."

"Should we swing by her house?"

"She's not there. If someone's following her, she must be in the car. I'm going to call Bridgette, that adjunct. She might know something."

Emily called the English department, hoping she'd find Bridgette. Luck was on her side.

"Bridgette, we're trying to find Sarah. Have you seen her?"

"Not today. She's usually in by now. Is something wrong? Sarah acted like something was bothering her when I saw her yesterday."

"I'm sure she's fine. I just needed to talk to her. If you hear from her, tell her to call us."

Susan said, "So maybe Dr. William Rowan has more to do with this than we thought. Do we need to make a trip to Michigan?"

"Susan, that's a little crazy. And what if Sarah reaches out to us again? We can ask the police to investigate though. We might as well turn around. Obviously Sarah isn't at school."

When they got home, Henry and Mike were out front looking at deer through binoculars.

"Did you find her?" asked Henry.

"No, but she called, and she's scared. She knows something about Ashley's murder. It has to do with that professor who went back to Michigan. That's what it sounds like."

"Hand me those binoculars," said Emily. She focused the binoculars on Kurt Olav and his companion. Again they were turned so their faces weren't clear. "I can't see her face, but that sure looks like Sarah. Was it him who was following her?"

"Let me see," said Susan. She grabbed the binoculars. "Oh no!"

"What? What?" said Emily.

"He's... She's..."

"Give me those," said Henry. "Oh, you're right."

"About what?" said the others.

"Kurt has her by the arm. She's trying to get into her car, but he's not letting her leave."

"Call 911. Come on, let's get over there," said Emily.

Henry grabbed his keys, and the others piled into the Jeep. Susan picked up a large branch that was lying in the driveway.

"What good will that do?" said Mike.

"It's better than nothing. We can't go over there unarmed."

Henry peeled out and zipped to Kurt's driveway where Kurt and the woman were still fighting.

Emily said, "Kurt, stop that. Let her go. Let Sarah go."

Kurt said, "What are you talking about?" The girl turned around. She was clearly not Sarah Kimberly.

"Emily said, "I'm sorry. We thought..."

"Thought what? This is my daughter, Chloe. I was trying to convince her not to leave though it isn't your business."

"Sarah Kimberly, the adjunct instructor at school... She's in trouble and we thought..."

Susan said, "She looks just like your daughter from the back."

Chloe said, "My Dad and I haven't spoken for years. I came out to tell him his wife, my mother, just died."

"Ex-wife. For years now," said Kurt. "She poisoned Chloe against me, and I wanted her to hear me out."

A patrol car pulled up, and an officer jumped out. "I got a call. What's the problem?"

Emily said, "I'm sorry, Officer. It was all a misunderstanding."

"Everything is fine," said Kurt.

The officer turned to Chloe for confirmation. "It's okay," she said. "This is my dad. He wasn't trying to hurt me."

After looking from one to the other, the officer left, and again Emily and Susan apologized profusely.

"This is family business. I thought by moving here, privacy wouldn't be an issue. Come inside, Chloe. Please."

Chloe agreed and followed Kurt into the house.

"We sure have egg on our faces now," said Susan.

Henry said, "You shouldn't have turned those binoculars on him in the first place, you know that. Come on, let's go home."

"But Sarah..." Emily wrung her hands.

"Why didn't you say anything to the police about Sarah?" said Henry.

"I... I was too wrapped up in thinking Kurt was with her. I'll call Detective Wooster right now."

Chapter 28

Emily and Susan huddled over the computer. The police said they wouldn't search for Sarah until she'd been missing twenty-four hours. It was up to them. Finding Sarah was urgent and the only clues they had were "professor" and "Midwest."

"Susan, I'm not finding anything other than what we saw before. Nothing in Professor Rowan's history points toward inappropriate behavior with students. Yes, he had a problem with alcohol, but it seems like he's coped with it and has held a steady job in Ann Arbor for years."

"Maybe she meant that he saw something."

"Ashley was murdered after he left. He wouldn't know anything."

"Let's fly out there and see."

Emily searched for flights to Ann Arbor. "It's kind of expensive."

Henry and Mike walked in. Henry looked over Emily's shoulder. "What's expensive?" He leaned closer. "Oh, don't even tell me. You're not seriously planning on flying out to talk to that professor are you?"

"Well, we were thinking about it. It's our only lead, and we have to find Sarah."

"That's ridiculous." Mike shook his head.

Susan said, "Just think if Lynette went missing. We'd do anything to find her. Her parents must be worried sick when they can't reach her."

"Her parents! Do you think she went home?" said Emily. "Let me see the computer. I have her home number on here somewhere." She clicked until she found it. "I'm going to call them now."

"You're going to scare them," said Henry.

"Not if she's with them." Emily made the call.

"Hello, Mrs. Kimberly. This is Emily Fox. I'm a professor at St. Edwards. I was wondering if your daughter is home by any chance."

"Home? Why would she be here? She's at school, isn't she?"

"I don't mean to scare you. It's just that we had a meeting scheduled and she didn't show. That isn't like her."

"No, it isn't. What if she's hurt? Did anyone go by her apartment? I'll get on the phone to her friends and see if anyone's heard anything."

"I'm sorry if I alarmed you."

"It's our daughter. Of course, we're alarmed though we appreciate the alert."

"We'll keep in touch. I'm sure she's fine."

After she'd hung up, Emily said, "They haven't seen or heard from her. As far as they'd known, she was here at school." She brought the conversation back to the Michigan trip. "We have tons of frequent flier points. Susan and I will run over there overnight and be back before you know it."

Mike said, "This isn't turning out to be much of a vacation. Susan, we're supposed to be spending time with our friends, not chasing murderers. This is supposed to be a break from your regular routine, not more of the same."

Susan kissed his forehead. "We'll be back before you know it. Meanwhile, you can enjoy ice-fishing and snowshoeing with Henry."

Emily added, "And you're welcome to stay here as long as you'd like."

"I'll have to go back to work eventually," said Mike. "But I know I'm not winning this argument."

Emily found a flight leaving the next morning. "We'll have to go through Detroit and rent a car, but we can still see him midafternoon." Emily called Dr. Rowan and set up a meeting.

"Emily, wasn't he suspicious about why we were calling?"

"Not at all. I told him I was writing a book about the Ashley Young case and that I was a professor at St. Edwards. As a matter of fact, he invited us over for dinner. Says his wife is a great cook."

"Wow, Midwestern hospitality. Let's swing by Sarah's place one more time before we buy the tickets."

Apartment complexes were unheard of in Sugarbury Falls. Instead, most temporary residents rented seasonal cabins or rooms. Many Sugarbury Falls residents picked up extra money by renting to students. Emily and Susan rode over to Sarah's apartment, which was a small shed-like structure behind a cabin.

"This place is falling apart. Sarah would have been better off renting a tiny house from Peewee Miniatures." Emily glared at her. "I was just kidding."

They knocked on the door.

"No one's here," said Emily. "Let's see if the owners are home."

They knocked at the main house and were greeted by a fortysomething lady in jeans and a cardigan. "Can I help you?"

Emily explained that they were looking for Sarah.

"I haven't seen her since yesterday."

"Was there anything unusual that happened recently? Anything out of the ordinary?"

"Come to think of it, she had a visitor. There was a truck parked outside on the grass. She never has visitors."

"Did you get a look at the visitor? Was it a man? Can you describe the truck?"

"I didn't see who it was. The truck was pretty run-of-the-mill looking. Dark color—blue or black. Later on before bed I peeked out the curtains and the truck was gone."

Wasn't it a truck that drove Emily's car into the lake? Susan thought. *Did she mean truck or van? If it was a van, it could easily have been Peter Taglieri's.*

"Thanks for your time." Emily handed the woman a card in case she remembered something later. They got back into the Jeep.

"Emily, think hard. Was it a truck or a van that chased your car into the lake?"

"Things are kind of a blur from that night. I thought it was a truck, but it could have been a van."

"I think we have no choice but to fly to Michigan. The police won't even start looking for her yet, and by the time they do, it may be too late," said Emily.

"Let's get packing. Michigan, here we come."

Chapter 29

The Detroit airport was buzzing with activity when Susan and Emily arrived the next morning. Several flights had been canceled overnight due to a severe snowstorm, and travelers, not in good moods, clamored to get available seats. Susan was grateful that they were arriving rather than leaving. She hoped the mess would be straightened out before their return flight left tomorrow.

"Car rentals are that way," said Emily, pointing toward the escalator. Susan followed her to the Avis counter where they'd reserved a Camry. Emily entered Dr. Rowan's address into her phone, and they headed for Ann Arbor. While driving, Emily received a phone call. It was Coralee.

"Emily, I'm sorry to bother you, but Noah remembered something that may be important. Sarah called in sick yesterday and didn't show up or call to say she wouldn't be here this morning. She's always been so responsible."

"I know. We're looking for her. The police won't take her disappearance seriously until more time passes."

"Noah said he remembered seeing her a few times talking to Peter Taglieri. He eats at the inn rather frequently."

"What did he say?"

"He was asking her about you. He wanted to know your schedule. He asked her about your book. Noah said he pulled out a wad of money and tried to hand it to her."

"Really? Did she take it?"

"No. Noah said she told him to get lost. Good for her. I'm sure it's more than she makes working a whole week here."

"Coralee, thanks for telling me. Hope things are going okay for Noah."

"His trial is coming up in a few weeks. The lawyer knows his stuff, but we're all nervous. I don't want to see him go to jail."

"Hang in there. Tell Noah we're thinking about him."

Emily relayed the conversation to Susan.

"We know Peter Taglieri has been involved in criminal activity in the past. Why would he need your schedule? He doesn't want you writing that book and discouraging potential mini homebuyers. Did he make a mistake, thinking he was killing you but killing Martha instead?"

"I don't get the grave on his property. He wasn't around when Ashley was killed." The GPS voice broke her train of thought. "Oh, well, we're almost at Ann Arbor. Let's focus on the task at hand first."

Ann Arbor was a beautiful college town, full of trees glistening with ice. Susan imagined how lush the streets must look in other seasons. Snowdrifts flanked the roads the snowplows had cleared after yesterday's storm. Emily turned into an older neighborhood on the same street as the university.

"This is it," said Emily.

She parked the rental car, and they walked carefully up the icy sidewalk. The two-story house was white with black shutters, guarded by what sounded like a ferocious dog. When the door opened revealing a Chihuahua smaller than her cats, Susan felt foolish.

"You must be Emily Fox. And this is your friend Susan Wiles, correct? I'm Harriet Rowan. Come on in, Bill is in here." She introduced them to her husband, a pleasant man, around Mike's age. Harriet brought out a pot of coffee and a coffee cake.

"I'm putting together a true crime book about the Ashley Young case, like I said on the phone. I know it's been almost a decade, but can you tell me what you remember."

"I don't remember a lot from that time. I was drinking heavily, having frequent blackouts. I'm embarrassed to admit."

Harriet said, "But he pulled himself together and hasn't had a drink since we moved here, right, honey?"

"I shudder when I think about my life back then," Rowan continued. "Thank God I got hooked up with Alcoholics Anonymous. I still go to at least one meeting a week. They saved my life."

"Do you have any idea who would have taken over your classes back then?" said Emily.

"There were two colleagues in the department who had room in their schedules. They gave the class to a woman named Maya Cavanaugh. Good woman, knew her craft. She was pregnant at the time. I don't know if she lasted the whole semester."

"Had you moved here to Ann Arbor before Ashley's disappearance?"

"No, I was still in town. Took me a while to get sober and search for a new job. They interviewed me, the police did. I couldn't even remember where I was when she went missing."

"Then a witness came forward," said Harriet. "A woman was out drinking at the same bar as Bill that night. She vouched for him being there."

"I can't remember who was or wasn't there, but I appreciate that she came forward."

"The police checked security cameras outside the bar," said Harriet. "They saw Bill leave at closing time, and they have footage of him passed out on a stoop across the street afterward."

"So you have an airtight alibi?" said Emily.

"It would seem so. Sorry I can't be of much help."

Susan and Emily checked into their hotel.

"I'm disappointed," said Emily. "This trip was a waste."

"Not really. We know Bill Rowan had an airtight alibi, and a pregnant lady took over his class. We also learned from Coralee that Taglieri was trying to pay Ashley to feed him information about you."

"So Taglieri, like we thought, is still a possibility for Martha's murder."

"And for whoever is threatening Sarah. Perhaps a professor or someone related to the Midwest. If that's what she said. The connection was awful. Maybe instead of Professor, she was saying Peter."

Emily tried calling Sarah again with the same results as she'd been having.

"Still not there. Let's grab some dinner. Maybe by the time we get home tomorrow we'll know more."

Chapter 30

The trip back to Vermont went smoothly. Mike and Henry were waiting at the gate when Emily and Susan, tired and hungry, arrived.

"So, did you find out where Sarah is?" said Henry. "Or who killed Martha and Ashley?"

"No, but Dr. Rowan has an airtight alibi for the night Ashley disappeared. And he has nothing to do with Sarah's disappearance, even though she mentioned professor and Midwest."

"Susan, you will both be interested in today's news. The police confirmed that the body—rather the skeleton—was, in fact, Ashley Young. The DNA results confirmed it."

"Henry, did they say anything else?" said Susan.

"Just that they are working on it and they assured the public that justice would be done."

"I hope they've started looking for Sarah by now. And something else. Coralee called Emily to say Noah remembered seeing Sarah with Peter Taglieri at the inn. He offered Sarah money to tell him Emily's schedule and anything she knew about the book."

"Ashley's DNA was found behind Taglieri's trailer. The news report mentioned that also," said Mike. "I'm sure the police are working on a connection."

By the time they got back to the house, Emily and Susan were exhausted. Henry ordered food from Coralee's and brought it back for dinner.

"Noah's trial is in two weeks if they don't settle before then," said Henry.

"I hope the judge goes easy on him. He lives with his mother, after all, and I'm sure he's smart enough not to steal from her guests again. Turn on the news while we eat. I want to hear what they have to say about Ashley's body."

Midway through dinner, Emily heard the name Ashley Young.

"Come on. We have to hear this."

The four of them gathered around the TV. Ashley's remains were still missing, but the reporter mentioned that clothing and blanket remnants were discovered.

"First the body is in a shallow grave behind Taglieri's trailer, then the killer moves it to your barn. Why?" asked Susan.

"It could have been the other way around," argued Emily. "Perhaps it's been buried in our barn all these years, and when the jewelry was found, the killer got nervous."

Henry said, "And either he moved it onto his own property…"

"Or," continued Mike, "he was trying to frame Taglieri."

As they were talking, the news cut to a cabin with an ambulance parked in front of it. The paramedics carried out a body on a stretcher, covered head to toe with a sheet.

"Oh God. Who is that?" said Emily.

"The reporter says it's an apparent suicide. They won't release the name until the family has been notified."

Emily said, "Sarah! I'll bet they found Sarah. I'm calling Detective Wooster."

If that's Sarah, why would she have committed suicide? thought Susan. *She was afraid for her life. She was hiding in order to save herself. This isn't a suicide. Without even hearing the rest, I'm sure it was murder.*

Within what felt like minutes, Detectives Wooster and O'Leary knocked on the door. Detective Wooster said, "What do you know about this girl Sarah Kimberly? She was an instructor in your department, correct?"

"Yes, and she's been missing. It's her, right? The body you found is Sarah Kimberly."

"We are not at liberty to discuss whether or not this is Sarah Kimberly," said Wooster. "We are simply looking for information to aid our investigation."

"I was supposed to meet with her," explained Emily. "She said she had something important to talk to me about. Then she missed our meeting. Later, she called and said she was scared someone was after her. God, no. Sarah, dead? Another murder?"

Susan said, "And she called a second time. Said something that sounded like *Professor* and *Midwest*. Or she could have said *Peter*, as in Peter Taglieri. Emily had a bad connection."

"She told me she had proof of who killed Ashley Young," said Emily. "We tried to tell your department she was missing, but according to policy, they couldn't search for her until forty-eight hours had passed."

"Her parents hadn't heard from her, and the woman she rented from hadn't seen her all day but says she saw a dark-colored truck parked in front of Sarah's apartment the night before. The truck was gone in the morning. Are you getting all this?" asked Susan.

Detective O'Leary had been busily typing into a tablet the entire time. She held it up and waved it at Susan. Emily collapsed into a chair. Chester, as if to console her, jumped on her lap.

"Detective, what was the cause of death?" asked Henry.

"You know I can't discuss details of an open investigation."

"Open? So you're not sure if it was a suicide. That makes sense. We know Sarah was afraid of someone. Why would she kill herself if she was trying to avoid getting killed?"

Detective O'Leary put away the tablet, and she and her partner walked toward the door.

"Did you tell her parents?" said Emily.

"We have informed the parents of the deceased."

Her poor parents, Susan thought. *They have to be devastated. The killer realized Sarah had proof he'd killed Ashley Young ten years ago. Sarah wasn't here back then. She had to have found physical evidence or maybe a confession... We need to look through her things. Emily and I should go to her apartment and look around before the police close it off.*

Chapter 31

As if she'd read her mind, Emily said, "Susan, the proof Sarah was talking about had to be in her apartment, right? I think we should have a look."

Henry put his hands on his hips and stood tall and authoritative. "You have no business going over there. The owner isn't going to let you in, especially now, knowing Sarah is dead."

"But she doesn't know Sarah is dead," argued Emily. "Remember they wouldn't release her name on the news. We have to go over there tonight."

"Then let us at least go with you," said Mike.

Susan answered, "We'll attract too much attention if we all go. Besides, the owner's already met Emily and me."

Despite continued protests from both men, the women hopped into the Jeep and drove to Sarah's apartment.

"Let me do the talking," said Susan. "I'm pretty good at this."

Emily parked in front of the farmhouse. "I don't see a car. And the lights are out. I don't think anyone is home." She grabbed a flashlight from under the seat.

They knocked on the door and confirmed Emily's suspicion.

Susan said, "I guess we have no choice. We'll have to get into her apartment without a key."

"You know how to do that?"

"How hard could it be?" She and Emily tried the door and front window, both of which were locked.

Then they walked around the back and saw a small screened patio. Inside the patio, they spotted sliding glass doors. The screen door was locked. "If we get inside the patio," said Susan, "I'll bet we can get in. The door to the house looks flimsy from here."

"How can we get inside the patio?" Emily pulled the handle to the screen door. "It's locked."

Susan tried tugging on the screen, but it was taut. She looked for holes but found none. "If we cut the screen, we can reach in and open the door."

"I have nail scissors in my purse. I'll be right back."

Susan shivered waiting for Emily to return from the car. *What are we even hoping to find? Think, Susan. Did she find a murder weapon? Ashley's death was so long ago... Maybe a confession from the killer? Yeah, right. She said she had proof. I hope her killer didn't take whatever proof she had with him.*

Emily came back. "Here you go. Let's cut this sucker." The open nail scissors fit perfectly through the screen. She made a few cuts and announced, "Voilà. We're in." She reached through the cut screen and unlocked the door.

"Now we have to get into the house." Susan tried the door into the kitchen. "It's locked."

"What about the sliding door?" Emily gave it a tug. "It's open! She probably hasn't come out to the porch all winter. I'll bet it's been unlocked for months."

Using the flashlight Emily had brought, they searched the kitchen.

"The refrigerator is full. If she was planning on committing suicide, why do a major shopping?" said Emily. "And look at the fridge door."

On the front of the refrigerator, Sarah had a magnetic dry-erase calendar. "She has plans sketched in for the whole month." She looked at the entries. "Carol Swift. She's a reporter for the local paper. Look, Sarah was going to meet with her tomorrow. She didn't kill herself."

"We were pretty sure she didn't," Susan affirmed. "The killer must have known she'd go to the police or the newspaper. That's why he killed her. Let's focus on the proof she talked about."

Emily tried getting into Sarah's laptop but didn't have a clue as to the password. "I don't even know her birthday or pet names if she has any back home. This is fruitless." Emily checked under the sofa and on the bookshelf. "I don't see anything."

Susan opened the coffee table. "Nothing that looks like proof or a suicide note."

"If she'd written a note, wouldn't she have left it at the scene? The police didn't mention a note."

"Let's check the bedroom," said Susan. They peeked under the bed and in the dresser drawers. Susan opened the closet. A briefcase in the back of her closet? This could be something. "Emily, look."

They rummaged through the papers inside. Susan said, "A rental agreement, a copy of what she's done on her dissertation so far, college loan papers, bank statements..."

"Now what?"

Before Susan could answer, they both froze. Headlights glared through the window. "Get down," whispered Susan. They held their breaths. The lights went off. They peered out the window. "It's a truck... or a van. I can't tell; it's too dark."

"Someone is following us," said Emily.

"Or they came to do what we're doing."

After a few minutes, the headlights turned on again. They heard the engine start up. Susan peeked through the curtain. "It's leaving. Whoever was here is gone."

"We should go too. There's nothing here. We can try her desk at school tomorrow."

"Okay. But we need to watch our backs in case the killer is onto us."

When they came within sight of Emily's house, Susan said, "What's going on?" She sniffed. "I smell smoke." Henry, Mike, and Kurt were gathered at the barn.

"It's the barn!" cried Emily. "It's on fire. Oh my God."

They jumped out of the Jeep and saw Kurt and Henry aiming hoses at the barn. Mike aimed a fire extinguisher and released white foam all over the side. Susan read ugly, red graffiti that someone had spray-painted across the entire barn wall.

"*This is your last chance*. Who would have written that?" She heard the fire truck siren and, although primed with adrenaline, took a deep breath and said, "Peter Taglieri."

Emily grabbed her arm. "Or the killer."

"Or," said Susan, "they're one and the same."

The firefighters had the fire under control quickly. "Good thing you guys responded so fast with the hoses and fire extinguisher," said one. "They slowed it down enough that it didn't do any real damage. It didn't even burn all the way through the wall."

Another firefighter said, "Looks like a real amateur job. Thank goodness."

Another siren blared through the darkness. Detective Wooster jumped out of the car and said, "Is everything under control? Was it accidental, or are we talking arson?"

The firefighter said, "Definitely arson. Amateur job."

"And look!" Susan pointed to the side of the barn. "If that's not a threat, I don't know what is."

Detective Wooster said, "When did you first notice the fire?"

"Emily and I were… out. As we pulled closer to the barn, I smelled smoke and saw the flames. The men were here first." *Please don't ask us to elaborate on the word* out, Susan prayed.

Detective Wooster turned to Henry. "What happened?"

"Kurt came pounding at our door. He noticed it first."

"I was out with Prancer, and I saw the flames. I heard a car speeding away. I ran right over. We grabbed all the hoses we could find, and Mike grabbed the fire extinguisher."

"Did you notice what kind of car it was? Did you see anyone?"

"No, Detective. I wish I could be of more help," said Kurt.

Henry said, "You saved the barn from being totaled. You were a tremendous help."

A tremendous help, thought Susan. *Funny how he's always around when something happens…*

Chapter 32

The next morning, Henry and Emily had waffles and bacon on the table when Susan and Mike woke up.

"You didn't have to go through all this fuss," said Susan. "I know you're exhausted."

"Helps keep my mind off dwelling on how serious this all is."

"Are you up for some more snowshoeing?" said Henry. "It'll get our minds off this while the police do their jobs."

Emily sat down at the table. "I want to stop by the office and go through Sarah's desk. It won't take long. When we get back, we'll do some snowshoeing."

Snowshoeing? My hand has barely healed from last time, thought Susan.

Susan was surprised by her ringtone. "It's my half brother, George."

She stepped into the living room. "George, is something wrong? Is Audrey okay?"

"If by *okay* you mean sane and rational, then the answer is no. Richard proposed. They're going to get married. We have to stop them."

"How is she so blind to his tricks? He's been freeloading off her, and if they get married, he stands to inherit the house and her portion of stock in the school."

"Oh, and you'll love this. I was over there yesterday, and right out on the kitchen table she had papers scattered all over. She'd been reading through a life insurance policy. Richard took out a million-dollar policy on her. This is straight out of *Dateline*."

"As soon as we finish up here, I'll fly down to Florida. Mike will have to get back to work, but I have an open schedule. We'll take care of it. Meanwhile, you have to stall her."

"I'll do my best."

My kids don't need me to parent them anymore, but my mother does. Crazy, Susan mused.

Emily said, "Is everything okay?"

"My mother is about to make a big mistake. When we wrap things up here, I'll have to fly down to Florida. Do you ever feel like you have to parent your own parent?"

"You don't know the half of it. After what happened with my sister, and then my father left, I've been the parent for years. My mom can't take care of herself. She's seeking out husband number three, trolling the church basements and senior centers, sitting in on everything from Al-Anon to bereavement groups."

"Isn't Al-Anon for families of alcoholics? I know you barely drink. I didn't realize your brother was an alcoholic."

"He's not! That's the point. God forbid she take care of herself for once."

"I didn't even know you had a sister."

Emily tensed from head to toe. "I don't want to talk about it."

Emily abruptly began clearing the table, signaling Henry to begin loading the dishwasher. They both insisted Susan and Mike relax and enjoy being the guests. Susan turned on the TV, and now that Sarah's parents had been notified, the news featured a brief story on her "suicide." She thought about Sarah's poor parents. Not only were they dealing with the loss of their daughter, now the media was announcing it was Sarah's own doing.

"Susan, are you ready to go?" Emily called.

Susan grabbed her purse. She and Emily drove to the college and entered the adjunct's room. It felt like déjà vu. *Weren't they just rifling through Martha's office not long ago?*

"This is her desk, and that's her bookcase. She has one of the drawers in the filing cabinet too." Emily searched through the desk while Susan found Sarah's files.

"Susan, look at this. It's a check made out to Sarah. Look at the signature."

"Peter Taglieri. And that's some hunk of change he gave her."

"It's dated a week ago, and Sarah hadn't cashed it. Do you think it was another attempt to get her to spy on me, like Noah said?"

"She didn't cash it. I'm sure she didn't agree to his offer."

Joe Sommers walked into the room. "Hey, what are you two up to?"

"We're just cleaning out Sarah's desk," said Emily. "I'd like to send Sarah's belongings to her parents."

"Poor girl. I spoke to her just the other day. Her dissertation was really coming along." He leaned over Emily's shoulder. "Anything interesting in there?"

"Just what you'd expect. Here's a framed picture of her with her parents. I'm sure that will mean something to them."

Bridgette came in and headed toward her own desk. She sniffled and patted her eyes with a tissue. She avoided eye contact with Joe.

"Bridgette, I'm sorry about Sarah," said Emily. "I know you were friends."

"Yes, but I wasn't a very good one. I should have known she was planning on killing herself. I can't believe it. She was a bit off her game the past few days, but suicide? I wish she'd have confided in me. Maybe I could have helped."

"Don't blame yourself," said Joe. "All of us who knew her could say the same. She must have had some deep issues." He put his arm around her, and she pulled away.

"If so, she kept them well hidden," said Bridgette.

"You know," said Susan, "the police are presuming it was suicide, but they've hardly begun their investigation."

Joe said, "What else would it be? An accident? Surely no one murdered her."

Bridgette blew her nose. "I just came in to get my laptop. Let me know when you hear about funeral arrangements."

Chapter 32

Emily fished her keys out of her purse. "Let's hurry home. The guys are expecting us to go snowshoeing."

Susan was hoping they'd forget about it. Maybe she could talk them into popcorn and a Netflix movie instead. On the way, her phone rang.

"Lynette, is everything okay?"

"Audrey called. She and Richard are engaged. Thought you'd want to know. She said she hadn't yet talked to you."

"She's probably afraid to. She knows how I feel about Richard. Anyway, George called me. He feels the same as I do. And get this. Richard took out a life insurance policy on Audrey! How classic. Audrey knows about the policy and still is going ahead with this."

"I definitely smell trouble. We should stall her. Tell her to have the wedding after Jason and I go to China to pick up our daughter."

"Have you gotten a match yet?"

"Not yet but hopefully any day now."

"Well, we're almost back at Emily's. We're going snowshoeing this afternoon."

"You've got to be kidding. You… snowshoeing, Mom? Remember when we took that hot yoga class together and it took three of us to untangle you?"

"I know, I know. I'm working on an alternate plan. Talk to you soon."

When Emily's cabin came into view, Susan spotted a police car parked in the driveway. *Oh no. What is it this time? I hope they're here just to follow up on the fire. Please, God. Don't let it be another murder.*

The first person they saw was Kurt Olav. He had Kiki and Buzz by their collars. The officer slapped handcuffs on them.

"Mike, what's going on?" asked Susan.

Henry stepped forward. "We got another threat. A note nailed to our door warning us to leave things alone. Kurt here caught Kiki and Buzz red-handed nailing it to the front door."

"I happened to be out walking Prancer, and I saw those two going toward the cabin, hammer in hand. I knew they meant trouble, so I called the police, and I nabbed them by the scruff of their necks. Well, it was more like the scruff of their jackets."

The officer led Kiki and Buzz into the squad car. Buzz yelled, "You were warned. Just because we're out of the picture, don't think you're safe."

"Kurt, you've proven to be quite the hero," said Susan. "You happened to be outside to notice someone breaking into the barn, you were on hand when the barn caught fire, and now today."

Emily said, "We sure got lucky having him as a neighbor. Kind of makes up for having Kiki and Buzz on our other side."

Kurt took Prancer home, while the others went inside. Henry had started a fire in the fireplace. He poked the logs and said, "Ready for some snowshoeing?"

Susan rubbed her hands together over the fire. "You know, it's a shame to leave this cozy fire. And I saw some of Emily's homemade gingerbread cookies on the kitchen counter this morning. How about we stay in and watch a movie."

Mike said, "I thought you wanted an adventure? Back home you couldn't wait to try cross-country skiing, ice skating…"

Emily interrupted him. "I think a movie is a great idea. I'll make some hot chocolate while you guys find a movie on Netflix." She went into the kitchen.

Henry added a log to the fireplace and flipped through the movie choices. "Comedy, drama, or action adventure?"

"How about a good mystery," suggested Susan. Mike shot her a look.

Susan and Mike snuggled on the sofa under the afghan. Henry and Emily sat in front of the fire on oversized cushions, Chester between them. While the movie played, the police called Henry's cell phone.

"The police said Kiki and Buzz admitted to making the other threats and to spray-painting the barn. Setting it on fire too."

"Really? That's great. At least we don't have to worry about them anymore," said Emily.

After the movie, Emily said, "How about some dinner?"

I'm stuffed to the gills with popcorn and gingerbread, but there's always room for Emily's cooking, thought Susan.

She and Mike chopped vegetables for the salad while Emily stir-fried chicken and vegetables in a wok. Henry set the table.

"I wish you'd both move here after Mike retires," said Emily. "It's so nice to have good friends around."

"You have Kurt," said Mike. "And Kiki and Buzz when they get out of jail."

"We'll see what the laws are around here. Those two might just end up with a fine and some community service," said Henry. "They can put them to work cleaning barns or shoveling manure from the fields.

That'll send them running back to the city so fast they won't care about selling to Peter Taglieri."

Emily's phone vibrated on the counter. "It's Coralee. I hope everything is okay." She walked into the living room.

Susan said, "I hope Kurt was able to reconcile with his daughter. Emily said she went back to Minnesota."

"Kurt won't tell us anything," said Henry. "He's a man of few words. We didn't even know he had a daughter or an ex-wife for that matter."

Emily returned and said, "You're not going to believe this. The police found the murder weapon. They found a pipe hidden in Peter Taglieri's trailer with blood on it. The blood matched Martha's."

"What made them get a warrant for Taglieri's trailer?" asked Henry.

"Coralee overheard two officers talking about it over dinner at the inn. They received an anonymous call. That paired with the grave... I guess that was enough for them to take notice."

"I hope they called Martha's sister. She'll be relieved to know the killer is in jail," said Susan. "I wonder if they'll be able to tie him into Ashley's murder. He didn't live here back then, but who knows? Maybe he had friends in the area and came for visits."

"The police will figure it out," said Mike. "Noah is no longer a suspect, and Emily's friend's murder is solved. Meanwhile, we need to be getting back to New York in a few days. The permits office won't wait on me forever. They've been more than flexible since my heart attack, and I don't want to feel like I'm taking advantage of them."

"And I guess I'll have to do something about Audrey. What a mess. The mother who adopted me, the one I call Mom, never would have fallen for Richard's nonsense. I miss her."

Emily put on a pot of coffee and cleared the table. "How about a game of gin rummy?"

"Okay, Emily, but I'm warning you. Mike always wins."

The fire died down, and after a few hours absorbed in playing cards, Susan fell into bed and slept solidly all night through.

Chapter 33

The next morning, Susan and Emily went for a walk while the men cleared the breakfast dishes. Gray clouds hung low, threatening snow. Susan wrapped her scarf around her neck more tightly.

"So how's your doctor-to-be Evan doing?" Emily asked. "I heard you talking to him on the phone while I was making breakfast."

"I'm so proud of him. He scored a 270 on his step one medical board exam. He should be able to get into the very best residency programs, according to Henry."

"That's wonderful. Has he chosen a specialty yet?"

"He's doing his first rotation. He says he'll decide after he gets nearer to finishing his third year. I hope he picks one on the east coast, preferably New York. St. Louis is far enough away. We hardly see him now."

"I hear you. I know I'm missing something by not having children."

"Why didn't you? You and Henry have always had solid careers. If you wanted to keep working full time, you could have hired a nanny or worked from home."

Snow fell in flurries, which rapidly became bigger, icy flakes. Susan nearly slipped on the newly wet road.

"I couldn't handle having a baby after seeing what we went through with my little sister. I still can't talk about it all these years later. It destroyed my mother's marriage, and I think it caused her to become the airhead she is today. It's snowing harder. Let's turn around."

Susan pulled up the collar on the new wool jacket she'd bought during her visit. She buttoned the top, and the gold button came right off into her hand. She looked down at it. *I've seen one like this recently. Where?*

"Susan, I'll sew that back on for you at home. They attach buttons so flimsily sometimes."

It's like the button I found when I fell snowshoeing, near the barn, Susan thought.

When they got to the end of the driveway, Emily checked the mailbox. "In all the excitement yesterday I forgot to get the mail." She sorted through the pile. "What's this? The return address says Sarah Kimberly." She pulled off her glove and tore it open.

Susan hung over her shoulder. "What is it?"

"It's a small key. Does it look like it's from a safety deposit box?"

"No, it's not the right size. And it's too small to be a door key." Susan took the key in her hand and examined it more closely. "It looks like it goes to a padlock."

"Did you see any padlocks when we were at Sarah's apartment?"

"No. I would have noticed. And I didn't see any in the TA office either."

They hustled into the house and showed it to Henry and Mike. Henry said, "It could be a lock she used on a bike or maybe a locker."

"They don't have lockers at the college?" said Mike.

Emily's phone vibrated. "It's from the school."

She said, "Bridgette. What's wrong? You sound upset."

"Something isn't right. I know in my heart Sarah didn't kill herself. Last night I remembered her mumbling something about *Ashley Young* and *professor* shortly before she died. She ran out of the office and said she'd explain later."

"Did she say anything else?"

"No, but I got to thinking. I wondered if Ashley had any of the professors who are here now. I asked Gerald Reynolds. He's been here since then, and he hangs around Morgan's office a lot so I've gotten to know him. He told me Ashley was one of Joe Sommers's students. Said Joe took over for some pregnant lady in the middle of the semester and his wife was glad they didn't dump the extra class on her."

"Gerald has dementia. Are you sure he was making sense?"

"I know sometimes he doesn't, but he was sharp as a tack during our conversation. I don't know if it means anything. Should I tell the police?"

"Yes, I think you should," said Emily. "It may be nothing, but it could be important. Let me know what they say."

Emily relayed the conversation to the others. Susan reminded Emily that Joe said he didn't know who took over and he didn't know Ashley. "Why would he lie?"

Before Emily could answer, Henry said, "Eureka! They do have lockers at school. In the fitness center. Did Sarah ever mention going to the gym?"

Emily thought for a moment. "Yes! I once saw her in leggings and a sweatshirt. She said she was heading to spinning class at the gym."

"Emily, let's go over to the gym and find that locker before it starts storming worse."

"They're forecasting a blizzard. You should both stay put."

"We'll be quick." She gave Henry a kiss. "Love ya."

Chapter 34

The two-story, state-of-the-art fitness center was a fairly new addition to the campus. It met the needs of almost any exercise aficionado, with an Olympic-size pool, an indoor track, rows of weight machines, racquetball courts, and a myriad of group exercise classes. Susan saw a sign advertising hot yoga, and she cringed.

"We at least should have worn gym clothes. It's bad enough we're old, but dressed in street clothes we stick out like sore thumbs," said Susan.

"No one cares. Besides, the gym is almost deserted. Guess everyone is worried about the Nor'easter they're predicting. Come on, the woman's locker room is over there."

Susan and Emily entered the locker room. One student was changing out of her workout clothing and soon left, leaving the entire area empty. There were three walls full of lockers, with changing benches in the center and showers off to the side. A door led directly to the pool area.

"Gyms have come a long way since I went to college," said Emily. "My school had a basketball court and a big empty room with varnished wood flooring where we could workout using our own videos. I still have my *Sweatin' to the Oldies* and Jane Fonda videos. Don't have a VCR anymore, but I couldn't just throw them out."

"I love Richard Simmons," said Susan. "And that Jane Fonda looks terrific for her age. Why don't you start with that wall, and I'll start with this one. Some lockers have combination locks at least. Narrows it down a little anyway."

Methodically they tried lock after lock, keeping an eye on the door. If anyone walked in and saw two women trying to open locker after locker, surely they'd call the police. The clinking of the locks against the metal became a rhythm of its own.

"This girl didn't even use a lock," said Susan. "She left these expensive Nikes sitting here for anyone to steal." Nikes, she thought. *Joe Sommers wore Nikes when we saw him and Bridgette hiking. There was a sneaker print by Emily's barn... It didn't belong to Noah.*

"I'm on the last row of this wall. I hope we're on the right track. Just because Henry says it could be a key to a gym locker, doesn't mean it is."

Joe Sommers. His coat was missing a button. Think hard, Susan. Yes, it looked a lot like the button I found by the barn when I fell off the snowshoes.

"Susan, I found it! Look. The key opened this locker."

Susan ran over to where Emily was. Emily pulled out a gym bag with Sarah's initials on it. She unzipped the bag. "A bathing suit, shampoo, flip-flops... just what you'd expect."

"Try the outside zippered part."

"Here. Photos."

"Let me see." Susan examined the top one. "It's a photo of a metal pipe, and there's blood on it! Detective Wooster said there were lead particles in Martha's hair."

"But they already found the pipe in Peter Taglieri's trailer."

"Sarah took a picture showing it in the trunk of a car, but she also was clever enough to take a picture of the license plate. The police can track this down easily. Sarah must have figured out who murdered Martha. Do you think it's Taglieri's plate?"

"No, he has that stupid vanity plate that says *TNY House*. I'm sure you noticed it."

"That's right, I do remember. Now, look at this other photo. It's a wall shrine to Ashley Young! Like you see on *Law and Order* or those serial-killer movies. See, there are newspaper articles about her death, the investigation, even one about your writing a true-crime book about the case. And several pictures of Ashley."

"Whose house do you think it is?"

"I don't know, but I'm sure the police can find it. Let's go show this to them."

Emily and Susan ran out of the gym. The snow was falling much more heavily than before. Emily had to scrape the snow off her windshield before they could pull away.

"Look, Susan. I have two text messages. I guess the service wasn't working inside the locker room."

"What do they say? Are they from Henry?"

Emily's face turned white. "Oh. My God. They're from Sarah! She says, *Faked death, hiding out. Help.* The second text says to meet her at the covered bridge. It's not far from here."

"But the police found her body!"

"Did they ever admit it was Sarah? She was covered with a sheet when they showed her on the news."

"They said her name eventually, but they could have been mistaken. They knew Sarah was missing so maybe they just assumed it was her. Let's go."

Emily slipped and swerved as she sped out of the parking lot. The windows fogged up, and Susan kept wiping the windshield off with her glove. They were barely out of the parking lot when they saw a car stuck on the ice. Under normal circumstances, Emily would

have tried to help but not now. They had to get to
Sarah, and they had to get there fast.

"Emily, do you think Joe Sommers is the killer?"

"Joe? Heavens no. Not in a million years."

"He was missing a button off his coat. It was just
like the one I found at the barn. And he said he heard
arguing outside his office window the day Ashley went
missing. He couldn't have heard anything with his
window closed, and it was stuck, remember? He said he
hadn't been able to open it for years."

"You're right, he did say that. And he didn't admit
to taking over the class when Dr. Rowan was fired. And
he told us Gerald and Morgan Reynolds came late to
the inauguration but we saw on the tape they were there
from beginning to end."

"He was trying to direct the investigation toward
them. Emily, watch out!"

Emily yanked the steering wheel just in time to
avoid hitting a car that momentarily lost control on the
icy road. "I'm going to have to slow down. We have to
reach Sarah in one piece."

"I just thought of something else. Remember how
Ashley's parents said they received a postcard from
Mexico?"

"Joe made a remark about Coralee's huevos
rancheros tasting authentic. He said he'd just come
back from Cancun. Susan, call Mike and the police.
Tell them where we're heading. It's the covered bridge
on Sweet Briar Lane."

Susan punched in Mike's number. "I don't have
service! Let me try your phone. No service either." She
threw the phone down in frustration. "Guess we're on
our own."

"There's the bridge up ahead." Emily pulled the car
over to the side of the road, and they ran to it.

"Sarah. Sarah, we're here! You're safe now. Come out! We got your message," cried Emily.

"We'll take you straight to the police station. Come out! We've got you," yelled Susan.

They entered the covered bridge, barely able to see between the gray sky and the dark bridge covering. Susan saw movement from the other end. Someone was coming toward them. "Sarah! We're so happy you're alive."

"Sorry to disappoint you, but it's not Sarah. Sarah's dead. I killed her myself."

Emily turned on the flashlight app on her phone and screamed. "Joe! What are you doing here? What did you do to Sarah?"

Joe came closer. "Sarah figured out that I killed Martha. She needed help changing a tire. I opened my trunk to grab my tools, not remembering I still had the murder weapon in it. Stupid mistake. I changed the tire for her. While I was doing it, she must have snapped a picture of the pipe. Later on she told me she had proof I killed Martha. I put two and two together."

"Why did you kill our colleague and friend? You and Martha had a nice relationship."

"I didn't mean to kill her. It was *you* I was after. I couldn't let you keep digging around in the Ashley Young case. I know you. You weren't going to stop until you figured it out."

"But why did they find the pipe in Peter Taglieri's trailer?" said Susan.

"Why do you think? I planted it there. The skeleton too. I had her safely hidden in your barn until that fool of a jewel thief, Noah Saunders, started poking around in there. I was afraid he'd find her. When I dug her up, there was nothing left but bones and clothing after all those years. I'd wrapped her in a blanket back when I first buried her. Good thing, or the bones would have spilled all over when I picked her up."

"So you dropped her scarf in the barn when you went to move her?"

"Yes, Susan. Emily's nosy neighbor went banging on the door asking if someone was in there. I had to get out in a hurry and didn't realize I'd dropped it."

The wind had picked up, and the bridge swayed slightly as Joe came closer. Susan's heart pounded. *His face is so evil-looking,* she thought. *His eyes are like coal. How are we going to get out of this? No one knows we're here, and the roads are so bad it's doubtful we'll run into anyone.*

Emily said, "Where's the body now? It disappeared from Taglieri's too."

"After they found the car, I knew the search would start up again. If they found the actual skeleton in the grave behind Taglieri's, they may have found trace evidence leading back to me. I moved her one more time. She's now in her final resting place."

Snow blew in from the end of the bridge. Joe stepped closer. The bridge swayed harder. Susan shivered as his menacing figure was now only inches from them.

"The police have the pictures Sarah left. They have proof, and it's only a matter of time," said Emily.

Joe laughed. "You never had a chance to bring those photos to the police. I followed you. You left the gym and came straight here. After I get rid of you both, I'll take the photos out of your car and destroy them. No one will be the wiser. I've already destroyed my shrine to Ashley back at my house. Damn Sarah found that too. I'd invited her over to talk about her dissertation. Those pretty young teachers are my fatal flaw, always have been. While I was on the phone, she must have been poking around and found it, again snapping pictures."

"How do you think you're going to get rid of us? It's two against one. Run, Susan."

Joe pulled a gun from his pocket. "Two against one, but one is armed. Let's go."

He got behind them and prodded them across the bridge with his gun until they were out in the snow once again. A rocky river bank greeted them. The freezing cold river water had a particularly strong current. The swishing sound of the water above the sound of the wind made Susan's head spin. *Think, Susan. We have to get out of this. If Emily and I ram into him, he won't be able to shoot us both. And his aim will be off.*

"Come on, ladies. You're about to join Sarah at the bottom of the river." He grabbed Emily. Susan prayed. *Hail Mary, full of grace... Our Father who art in heaven... Please help us.*

As Joe was about to wrestle Emily off the river bank, sirens blared behind them. Detectives Wooster and O'Leary jumped out of the squad car, guns in hand, startling Joe. Susan grabbed the gun out of his hand, surprising herself as well as her friend. O'Leary snapped handcuffs on Joe Sommers and read him his rights. Seconds later, Henry and Mike jumped out of the Prius and ran to them.

"Emily, what were you thinking? I told you not to go out. This is the second time I almost lost you." Henry hugged her to his chest.

Mike said, "You know better. Wait till I tell Lynette about this one."

"How did you know where to find us? I tried to call, but the phones didn't have a signal."

Henry said, "We owe it to Kurt once again. He was coming home with storm supplies when he passed our

Jeep heading toward the bridge and found it suspicious. With the storm, he couldn't figure out why you were heading away from home, so he came over and told us he'd seen you. Of course, I figured you were in trouble and called the police right away."

"Let's go home. All I want to do is change into dry clothes and curl up in front of the fire."

"Home it is. Maybe after you girls rest, we can make it over to Coralee's for dinner. The weatherman says the storm is moving out. Look, it's already stopping." A sliver of sunlight broke through the gray clouds. "By the way, I have a surprise for you. It's in the barn."

Chapter 35

"Close your eyes," said Henry. He led Emily to the barn, followed closely by Mike and Susan. *I bet he bought her a horse. She'll be so happy,* Susan thought.

"One, two, three, open your eyes."

Emily screamed and threw her arms around Henry. Then she opened the door and crawled inside her brand new, shiny silver Audi Quattro. "I love it! You know I've always wanted one of these."

"Your other car was totaled, and I know how much you hate sharing." Henry smiled and got into the car beside her. "It's got all-wheel drive, great for the weather around here. You can start it from inside the house so the heat gets going before you get in. And it has seat warmers."

"I love it. Guess we'll try it out on our way to dinner tonight."

* * * * *

Later that evening, the inn was full of diners happy to escape being trapped at home by the weather. Susan smelled biscuits, and her eyes scanned the dishes that the other diners were eating, knowing it would take her a while to decide amongst all the fabulous choices. Coralee led them to their usual table.

"I'm glad you and Susan are safe and sound. I can't believe you caught the killer, Joe Sommers. He came in here all the time to eat. I never would have guessed. He seemed like such a nice man."

"Like Detective Wooster said, killers come in all shapes and sizes. And to be successful criminals, by nature they have to be sneaky and deceptive." *Oh no,* Susan realized. *Here I go again putting my foot in my mouth.* "Coralee, I wasn't talking about Noah."

"It's fine. The lawyer worked out a deal. Noah won't be spending any time in jail. The things he chose to steal didn't add up to enough to be considered grand larceny. He has a huge fine to pay, and, of course, he returned all the jewelry to its owners. It goes without saying I'll be working him so hard he may wish he was in jail!"

Emily said, "That's great, Coralee. I think Noah has learned his lesson."

All four buried their noses in the menus. Every dish looked mouthwatering. They all settled on the filet mignon with truffles and scalloped potatoes. Susan had already eyed the desserts. *Red velvet cake or Oreo pie? Maybe both. It's been a tough day.*

Coralee brought a platter of mini chicken potpie appetizers to the table. "On the house. To celebrate good things yet to come. Noah's home and won't be going to jail. Peter Taglieri left town the minute the police released him. And I'm planning to renovate the bedrooms in this place one at a time as I can afford it. What's in your futures?"

Henry said, "The local hospital asked if I'd work part-time for them. They're severely understaffed. I was already starting to miss medicine."

Emily said, "I have an idea for a summer writing camp for adults. The college already said I could use their facilities. It will give writers a chance to focus on their craft without the everyday responsibilities they have back home."

"That sounds wonderful," said Susan. "I'm going to head to Florida to thwart my mother's wedding plans. Then I'm going to spend lots of time with my granddaughter and help Lynette get ready for the new baby."

Susan glanced at her phone and noticed a new text message. "Speaking of grandbabies, look! They matched Lynette and Jason with a baby. She sent a picture!"

Susan's mouth gaped open at the sight of her beautiful new granddaughter. "Look how precious. She's only three months old, and her Chinese name is Meilyn."

"How gorgeous. Look at all that hair! When do they bring her home?"

"Lynette said it takes about a month after they match a family with a baby. They go over with a group of other adoptive parents."

"The potpies are good, but this requires champagne." Coralee fetched a bottle of champagne and uncorked it at the table. "A toast to family, friends, and exciting adventures yet to come."

THE END

ABOUT THE AUTHOR

 Diane Weiner is a veteran public school teacher and mother of four children. She has enjoyed reading for as long as she can remember. She has fond memories of reading Nancy Drew and Mary Higgins Clark on snowy weekend afternoons in upstate New York and yearned to write books that would bring that kind of enjoyment to her readers. Being an animal lover, she is a vegetarian and shares her home with two adorable cats and a little white dog. In her free time, she enjoys running, attending community theater productions, and spending time with her family (especially going to the mall with her teenage daughter and getting Dairy Queen afterwards). *Murder is Collegiate* is Book 7 in her Susan Wiles School House Mystery series.